A hit team is
in the States

Both men were now jogging at full s...

Then it happened.

Bolan knew they were too late.

The night air erupted with the hellfire roar of a Russian-made RPG-7, and a fractured second later the guardhouse went up with a thunderclap that lifted the roof off the building and blew out the windows in an explosion of roiling flame. It blasted glass and wood and human bodies into the sky.

Then silence.

Death had blistered the hills and valleys of this walled-in slice of Maryland. And one of the forces here—the Iranians, the Mafia, Mack Bolan— would retaliate immediately and unmercifully.

For Bolan, this whole mission was vigilance over a nest of vipers.

Now he would be the next to spit venom.

There are plenty of devices for shunning death in every kind of danger if a man sticks at nothing in word or deed. But . . . the difficulty does not lie so much in avoiding death as in avoiding dishonor. For she runs faster than death.

–*Socrates*

Dishonor is, in itself, a form of death; in the end, the worst form, because it degrades the soul. We take to God only what we give to Life. I will not give it dishonor.

–*Mack Bolan,*
The Executioner

MACK BOLAN

THE EXECUTIONER 42

The Iranian Hit

DON PENDLETON

A GOLD EAGLE BOOK FROM
WORLDWIDE

TORONTO • LOS ANGELES • NEW YORK • LONDON • PARIS • SYDNEY

To those in the diplomatic community throughout the world, in embassies in every land, who work in good faith and with great courage to keep the world order intact without the use of weapons.

First edition published in May 1982

ISBN 0-373-61042-4

Special thanks and acknowledgment from the author to Stephen Mertz for his contributions to this work.

PROLOGUE

There were times when it would seem to a rational man that the whole world had gone crazy. But Mack Bolan knew that it had not. There were a lot of crazy people, sure—and even a few lunatic nations; these could not, however, state the case for the planet earth. The state of the planet was complexity, not insanity. Complexity, Bolan knew, was a natural consequence of growth. As the world's human population increased, and as individuals within that population continued to expand and evolve into smarter and more perceptive humans, then the problems of living together on this crowded earth increased geometrically—sometimes with quantum leaps.

The problem, as Bolan saw it, is that we do not all expand in the same direction, at the same time, or from the same stimuli. Equality between individuals was a political idea—and one not in conformity with natural law. The jungle knew better. All of man's great social inventions were, after all was said and done, a mortal attempt to repeal the laws of nature.

Anomaly. There was a word popularized by the space scientists (who had their own ideas about how to deal with natural law). *Anomaly*. It had to do with events that had not been planned, or intended. . .things existing outside the established order, something irregular or abnormal.

Abnormal was another word for *crazy*. So maybe that was why so many people were arriving at the conclusion that the world was headed that way. But it was not. Actually, the world was *anomalous*, a natural product of abnormal expectations in the human mind. The world of men was not a fixed system. It was not of a single piece but composed of many individuals and diverse elements, classes, types. Therefore, anomalous—because everyone expected everyone else to think and feel and view the world precisely as (or within narrow limits, the same as) he or she did. The world was not crazy, nor was it endowed with a natural sameness. And that was the problem for mankind. In complexity, things were never equal.

Men who could discuss learnedly the chemical composition of a distant star occupied the same time and space as aboriginal peoples who believed that star to be a tiny light imbedded in some celestial web suspended just beyond the earth. Men who right now were devising exotic environmental systems for human colonies in space share the planet with others who devoutly insist that man's adventures upon the moon were actually filmed in Hollywood as some godless hoax upon the world.

Anomalies, sure. They sprang naturally from the conflicting world views held by individuals who were not, in any sense, equals. If a man or woman is the sum total of all his or her experiences, how then can there be any claim of sameness between a Nobel physicist and an Australian bushman—or, for that matter, between a Beverly Hills housewife and her counterpart in Karachi. How do you get these widely disparate individuals to share a common world view when their basic thought processes do not follow the same track? More than a difference in language, or even in social cultures, the difference that divides is a conceptual chasm: the one simply cannot communicate with the other except toward the most elemental biological needs.

So...back to Square One. The world is not crazy. Its parts simply do not understand one another. And these parts need not be geographical divisions, particularly. The parts may exist side by side within the same city or village—within the same family, even. The parts are called human beings—and each is awfully isolated from everything else that exists, totally alone in the jungle of survival and crying out that "the world" has gone crazy because *anomaly* is the order of the day.

An anomaly can occur only where some specific expectation exists. An expectation is a human invention, usually born somewhere outside the jungle. It often finds form as an attempt to repeal some natural law while clothing itself as conventional wisdom.

Now and then, however, the expectation is no more than jungle law masquerading as moral order—and here is where anomaly ends and "crazy" begins.

Mack Bolan knew all about crazy, too. He did not live in the anomalous world. Bolan had dwelt all his adult life in the jungle of survival. . . and he knew its ways.

1

He sensed something about to happen from the moment his peripheral vision caught movement in the shadows shrouding the base of the high brick wall.

Bolan slowed the black Corvette to coasting speed and glided past, trying to discern exactly what had caught his attention. Then he saw her. A woman, moving furtively in the twilight, carefully picking her way along the wall that surrounded this estate in Potomac, Maryland.

The lady was a looker; it was clear even from a moving car on an evening road. Bolan registered shoulder-length blonde hair that seemed to shimmer even in the gloom, and a damn fine set of curves wrapped in a belted leather jacket against the October chill.

Then he was past her.

The woman moved at a quick clip in the opposite direction, still hugging the shadows of the wall. Still furtive.

Uh huh.

Mack Bolan sensed something. Something

ominous. Coupled with the fact that this wall bordered and protected the forty acres of ground that was Mack Bolan's destination. . . .

He let the Corvette roll another twenty feet, then steered to the shoulder and killed the engine.

Mack Bolan (a.k.a. Colonel John Phoenix) was togged for night work. The heavy dark sweater and navy pea jacket, worn over a nylon-weave Kevlar protective vest, were complement-ed by dark jeans and shoes. The silenced 9mm Beretta Belle was leathered under his left armpit beneath the jacket. Big Thunder, the mighty .44 Magnum Autoloader, rode low on his right hip, western-style. A leather attaché case within easy reach beside him carried a variety of hard-punch munitions and a full set of belted knives and garrotes. Snug in the compartment behind the Corvette's bucket seats were an infrared Star-tron spotting scope, an Uzi 9mm submachine gun, and a M1 match rifle sheathed in its leather case. Bolan was loaded for bear.

But he was not pleased with this latest mis-sion, and it hadn't even begun yet. He was in civilian territory with all of this hardware. The peaceful environs of upper-class rural Maryland dozed around him in the evening stillness.

Bolan hated bringing his war near civilians and avoided it at all costs. But this time the choice was not his. This hellground had been chosen for him. And so here he was, tooling through the darkening byways of the Potomac, loaded down with implements of death and destruction for the battle royal that was due to commence amid this quiet, rustic backdrop.

Within the next few hours.

That was the time element that Hal Brognola had passed on, and the initial intelligence data had been confirmed.

A few short hours. But Bolan knew that a hell of a lot could go down in much less time. The complications seemed to be starting already. Right. It promised to be *that* kind of mission. It was the only type of mission that a man of Bolan's capabilities ever drew.

So the big warrior's battle senses had all been on high as he approached the walled property.

That was how he spotted the woman.

The main entrance to the property was another half-mile up and around a corner from the direction in which the lady was heading. But Bolan had shifted his priorities. He reached behind the Vette's bucket seat and withdrew the Startron spotting scope, which was fixed with a window support clamp. He focused behind him on the woman. He couldn't shake his sixth-sense premonition that something was about to happen....

She was still moving away from him at a fast clip along the base of the wall. She seemed too caught up in her own thoughts to have noticed him slow down and pull over. For brief seconds—the one time she glanced back over her shoulder, still not at him but in the general direction of the high, imposing wall—he caught a stunning vision of high-cheekboned loveliness in the scope's greenish glow.

That beautiful face wore an expression of pure, naked terror.

A four-year-old Datsun entered the Startron's field of vision and braked to a stop at the curb near the woman. Bolan implanted the license number in his memory, then shifted his attention to the youthful-looking guy in his mid-thirties who leaped out from the driver side of the Datsun and dashed directly toward the lady.

Bolan felt himself tensing. He wondered what this confrontation he was witnessing was about. Did it concern his mission?

He relaxed.

There was no danger to the blonde from that quarter. No danger at all. The man and woman met in a passionate embrace and a long, soulful kiss. Then the guy took her hand and led her back toward the car. She accompanied him willingly, taking time for only one more apprehensive look over her shoulder at the wall.

Bolan pulled back from the scope, relieved that this was a false alarm. Now he could be on his way and about his business. About the mission. He only had a few short hours. And those numbers had already started falling, even before he'd been sent in on this job. But the coming confrontation was to be *inside* that walled estate. Not out here. Not playing voyeur on some girl from the household or staff who had chosen this moment and this place for a romantic assignation. Bolan would rather have all civilians out of range anyway.

He began unscrewing the Startron's window clamp when everything changed. And Bolan suddenly knew that this *was* the time.

Yes, by God.

He heard a loud squeal of braking rubber back up where the couple were and brought his eye back to the scope.

A '78 Malibu had swerved into the curb, blocking in the Datsun's front end. Four big dudes came barreling out of the Malibu and charged the couple on the sidewalk. The guy with the woman swung away from her to meet the onslaught, shielding her with his body. Then he died. Silenced saffron flashes licked out at him from four different angles, and the way he fell told Bolan that the man was dead when he hit the pavement.

Two of the hefties stooped and lifted the body, toting it back toward their car.

The other two grabbed the woman before she

could run, also dragging her toward the Malibu.
The blonde fought and twisted wildly in their
grip, but it did her no good. She was their pris-
oner.

Bolan was already swinging into action, toss-
ing the Startron into the compartment behind
his bucket seat and gunning the Corvette to life.
He stomped on the gas pedal, tugged the steering wheel, and brought the sports car around in
a fishtailing U-turn that momentarily included
the opposite grassy shoulder.

Only seconds had passed, but even as he
straightened the Vette out from the turn, Bolan
could see that the four men had moved with
stopwatch precision. The man's body and the
woman had been loaded into the Malibu. The
heap executed its own U-turn and sped off into
the distance.

Mack Bolan was a seasoned, savvy warrior.
He had baited many traps of his own during his
career as a soldier, both in Vietnam and against
domestic foes and world terrorism, and he was
fully aware that this could be a diversion intended to draw him away from the estate. There was
that chance, sure. But that wasn't Bolan's reading. The woman's struggles and the fear in her
face had been too real. The way the slain man
had fallen—yeah, too real.

One human being was dead.

Another was in obvious, serious peril.

Bolan saw no choice in the matter. The mission would have to wait.

The Malibu negotiated a corner a quarter-mile up the road and, its tires screaming, skidded out of view into the moonlit evening.

Bolan fed the Vette more gas and eased into third. The sports car's gears shifted with a smooth, purring sound like that of some living thing.

With lights off, Bolan tailed the Malibu around the corner onto another rural stretch that a street sign told him was Persimmon Tree Lane. The Malibu's taillights winked at him from a quarter-mile down the road. The driver had slowed down to legal cruising speed. Bolan decreased his own speed accordingly, holding his position at the quarter-mile mark, still running blind.

Apparently the guys in the Malibu didn't know they were being tailed.

Sure.

Unless it was a trap.

The track continued south on Persimmon Tree, out of estate country, through an area of ritzy developments that bordered the road, and finally into the grassy, hilly outer reaches of Maryland suburbia.

Bolan saw plenty of spots along the way that would have been ideal for hot contact with these boys, had this been taking place under ordinary circumstances. But the idea here was to save the lady's lovely hide, not expose it to the vagaries of a firefight. He would have to wait and choose his time and place carefully.

The Malibu swung east onto MacArthur Boulevard, a principal suburban artery that was lined with darkened businesses at this hour. But vehicular traffic was still heavy enough to finally warrant flicking on the Corvette's headlights. Bolan dropped back another few car lengths to compensate and held steady. No need to be on top of them, as long as they were in sight.

He reached behind him and grabbed the Uzi. The weapon was equipped with an enlarged, extra-capacity magazine, fastened at a right angle for speed and quick reload. Bolan knew that when he engaged these men, he would need to move fast, with maximum hard punch. The Uzi, with its relatively moderate rate of fire and its accuracy in open spaces, was perfect for the job. The odds would still be stacked; the lady's safety was still on the line (whoever the hell she was). But there would be no dicking around when Bolan took on these four—whoever the hell *they* were. None at all.

Both cars were moving smoothly in and out of the sparse traffic now, continuing east on MacArthur. With the Uzi nestled beside his right hip, Bolan next snatched up the small

UHF radio transceiver attached to his belt, which kept him in contact with home base.

Stony Man Farm, the 160-acre nerve center of Mack Bolan/John Phoenix's "new war," was a mere ninety miles to the south, in Virginia's Blue Ridge country. As usual, there was a team sitting back there at this very moment, doing overtime on this mission. A beauty named April Rose and a damn good buddy and head fed named Hal Brognola, waiting to assist or supply backup at the sending of an S.O.S.

Bolan did not feel the necessity of bringing in reinforcements, but Stony Man had to be told. They could relay word to those awaiting Bolan in the house back within those walled-in grounds—to the people Bolan had been on his way to protect. At least the estate had its own security force, which had served adequately—up until now. They would have to hold on a bit longer.

Before Bolan could make contact, however, the car up ahead accelerated with a sudden, unexpected burst of speed and skidded into a sharp right, zooming off the highway and out of sight amid a cluster of tall white oak.

Bolan dropped the radio and threw caution to the wind, sending the Corvette speeding in pursuit, wheeling onto the narrow blacktop road only seconds behind the first car.

A sign went zipping by to his right: Chesapeake & Ohio Canal National Park. Lock 17 Parking Lot.

The road curved and dipped up ahead. The Malibu's taillights were nowhere in sight. Bolan decreased his speed slightly, but continued on. So they were leading him toward the old canal and the Potomac River a few yards beyond. The river, with its strong undertow, would be ideal for disposal of an unwanted body. But the Malibu's destination was not to be that obvious. The narrow, seven-mile-long park was deserted at this hour and there were plenty of spots for an ambush.

They were waiting for him at the base of the first rise, just beyond a short underpass that cut beneath a stretch of old railroad track that ran along the canal's bank. They must have spotted him along that stretch of MacArthur, despite his precautions. Now they were parked at the point where the road widened for a parking lot. They obviously intended to zap the Corvette as it came out through the underpass. But they had not taken into account the glint of moonlight off the Malibu's chrome. Or the fact that their target was approaching from high ground. *Or* the capabilities of the man behind the Vette's wheel. Now it was too late.

Bolan tromped on the gas pedal and surged forward into the fray, again with lights off.

They were waiting for him. But they were not

ready for him. Just before the underpass, Bolan yanked the wheel to the right. The sleek black sports car left the road and went sailing up the side of the embankment. Bolan kept the hammer down. Railroad tracks clattered underneath; then the car overshot and was momentarily airborne before coming to rest with a four-point landing and skidding to a halt slightly beyond and below the waiting ambush car.

Bolan grabbed the Uzi and catapulted out from the Corvette's passenger side, his black garb molding him to the darkness.

Two of the guys had been leaning across the Malibu's hood, taking aim at the underpass with handguns, while a third had been pointing a pump shotgun over the trunk. Number Four must have been down out of sight, holding onto their captive. Now they spun around as one to meet this unexpected maneuver, and one of the handgun boys even had time to pull off a wild round before Death came for them.

Bolan squeezed off only a short burst from the Uzi, but it was enough to take all three men in a withering hail that stitched from left to right at upper-chest level, the Uzi's muzzle flashes illuminating the darkness like some unholy strobe light.

Dead bodies were still jerking and falling when motion erupted from the nose of the Malibu. Bolan had sized it correctly. Heavy Number

Four had been pinning the girl. Now he was straightening, forgetting about the blonde as he pawed for hardware beneath his jacket.

The woman kept her head. She dashed from the man's side, losing herself in the night.

The guy had his weapon halfway out when the Uzi burped again, almost discreetly. The force of the 9mm rounds smashed the man back against the car; then he pitched forward onto the grass alongside the road, his right hand still reaching under his left arm in a final statement of purpose.

The sudden silence was absolute. The car, the bodies—Bolan could see no sign of the lady.

Cautiously, he approached.

Wondering, as he did, just what the hell had gone down here.

Wondering about the mission.

Wondering what would happen next.

2

The mission was not supposed to be a complicated one. Nor an easy one, no. Not easy by any stretch of the imagination. But cut and dried, just the same.

Brognola had briefed Bolan only ninety minutes earlier. Bolan could still hear the cigar-chewing head fed's words.

"The man's name is General Eshan Nazarour," Brognola had told him. "An Iranian. High ranker in SAVAK, the Shah's secret police, until the revolution came along. The general lost both legs in a mortar attack on SAVAK headquarters during the final days of fighting, but he still managed to get out alive, which a lot of 'em didn't. For the last nine months, he's been lodged incognito on a forty-acre spread up in Potomac. He's got influential ties with plenty of big money in this town, and some of that money has been putting him up. But legs or no legs, the guy's a mobster, plain and simple, and the administration doesn't want anything to do with him.

"His visa expires at midnight tonight. He's sticking it out until the last minute, hoping his lawyers will be able to pull some strings—which they can't. The kicker is that we learned today that Nazarour has been marked for death by an Iranian assassination squad. At any time from now on. Any time today or tonight.

"Now we all know what it's like to have a foreign hit team prowling the country. It makes people edgy, right? But this time around we have hard data on the bastards and we're going to get them.

"The squad is a fourteen-man paramilitary commando unit—the best they've got—and they've been on his trail ever since January '79, when Khomeini's government took power. During the first week of trials, Nazarour was sentenced in absentia to death, on charges of 'torture, massacre of people, treason, and earthly corruption,' and our intel says he's guilty as sin of those charges and a whole lot more. So this hit team wants him bad.

"I don't know how they tagged him here, but our spook in Tehran reports that they picked up his scent the day before yesterday. The agent gathered the intel after the team had already been dispatched from Tehran—they left within two hours after learning of the general's whereabouts. They've probably been in D.C. most of today, reconnoitering and setting up the operation.

"This won't be their first hit, either. The team is led by a man named Karim Yazid, who made quite a bloody rep for himself with the *Cherikhaye Fedaye Khalq*—People's Sacrifice Guerillas—in Iran before the revolution. The group was trained by Libyan military personnel, financed by a radical Palestinian group, and was the toughest in the Mideast. Yazid drew from the *Cherikhaye Fedaye Khalq* when he put his present outfit together.

"So far, they've racked up a total of thirty kills in the past three years of Khomeini enemies around the world. Four in the Mideast, ten in Europe and sixteen—count 'em, sixteen—here in America. That's what's got the CIA and the other agencies asking us for help. We've advised Nazarour of our intel, and he's gone stone hard. He's been paranoid as hell the whole time he's been here, and I got the feeling after talking to him on the phone that he suspects this of being some sort of American trick.

"He's refused to allow any of our troops or security personnel onto the grounds. But he has agreed to allow Colonel John Phoenix to act in an advisory capacity to his own security staff.

"As I say, he has his suspicions, but he's not taking any chances in case our information is on the level. He's aware of this hit team, of course, and fully appreciates their capabilities. He's being guarded by a private security agency provided by one of these big-money friends of his, but he must know that better security than he's got hasn't kept Yazid's outfit from hitting effectively in the past. And he certainly knows that his 'protection' wouldn't stand a chance against this team in the dark.

"So he's refused to budge from the grounds of that estate until dawn. Which is fine with us. Striker, that hit team *must* attack tonight. Either at the place in Potomac or just after dawn, en route to the private airstrip in Rockville where Nazarour is planning to catch a plane out of the country. If they don't hit tonight, they run the risk of having the general slip through their fingers and disappear again, as he's done a few times in the past.

"So that's your mission. These assassinations have got to stop. All sorts of Third World hoodlums are starting to think they can march into this country and turn it into a shooting gallery whenever they please.

"When that hit team does launch their attack tonight, you'll be there to take them on. Sure, no one would cry if they did hit Nazarour, but the guy is excellent bait, and it's just too good a setup to pass by. The odds are stacked, but with Nazarour refusing to let us onto the grounds to protect him in force. . . well, your name is the only one in the hat, buddy. When that attack comes, do what you can. It's up to you. The top man says hit teams call for Phoenix.''

It was quite a speech. Brognola had spoken those words that afternoon, only hours after a bone-weary Bolan had arrived back at Stony Man from Minnesota. That mission had sapped him to his very soul—mentally, physically, and emotionally. And now it was to be Potomac, Maryland.

There had been time to requisition the necessary ordnance, time for a change into night clothes, time to pick up the cassette with additional background on the mission, to be absorbed on the drive to Potomac. And time to be gone.

There had not been time for any personal words with Brognola or with April, that bright-eyed lovely with the genius IQ, who was both ''warden'' of Stony Man Farm and the most important lady in Bolan's life.

During Hal's briefing, Bolan could tell that April, sitting on the sidelines, had things she wanted to tell him. Important things, like how glad she was to see her man back from Minnesota in one piece. Bolan could read that much from those brown eyes, which could express so much without words. But those eyes also said that she understood that the mission came first. The mission always came first. April was, yeah, that kind of special lady. She would tell Bolan the important things—the man/woman things that existed only for the two of them—when she saw him again.

Bolan hadn't had time to listen to the full tape that Stony Man's computer wizard, Aaron "The Bear" Kurtzman, had compiled from the general's dossier, but he digested the particulars. And he didn't like any of them.

Bolan knew that since the revolution, Washington had welcomed any number of the Shah's regime into the country, especially those interested in someday restoring some kind of sanity to a homeland being systematically driven back into the Dark Ages by a religious madman.

But Nazarour did not fall into this category. The man was as self-serving as he was ruthless, with nothing save his own shadowy interests at heart. Bolan understood that the Shah's rule had been far less than perfect, and Nazarour epitomized the corruption that had been one of the regime's continuing problems. A man with untold millions pillaged from his years as a top-echelon officer in what the Shah's military had perverted into one of the most dread secret police agencies in the world. Yeah, that was Eshan Nazarour. The man sounded like Savage incarnate.

But whatever else the general was, he would indeed be perfect bait for the trap Bolan hoped to spring when Karim Yazid's hit team came calling.

The world was growing smaller in many ways. There were fewer and fewer places where men could gather and talk of freedom and peace and plans for a better future without yesterday's mistakes. America was one of those places, and it had to remain so. If not for Eshan Nazarour, then for his countrymen who were more honorable than he, who cared about their Iran and dreamed and, yes, plotted for a day when freedom—real freedom—would ring in that torn land.

And not just the Iranian exiles, but those from Afghanistan and anywhere else in the world where the flame of freedom had been extinguished. These men, good and true, had to be reassured that America was safe and open to them. That their dreams and plans for a better world could be nurtured in safety. That they could seek asylum here from those merchants of terror and violence who saw fit to ignore all conventions and rules of diplomacy or morality.

No, Bolan had no love for cannibals of Nazarour's type. Bolan was glad the guy was getting booted out of the country on his tail. He deserved no less. But if protecting Eshan Nazarour for the coming few hours and protecting the values and rights that made this country great were one and the same thing, then, yes, Bolan was ready to take on whatever the Iranian hit force could throw at him, and return it in kind.

There was far more at stake here than the life of one corrupt ex-military man.

Bolan had been thinking about that as he'd approached Nazarour's temporary residence in Potomac.

That was when he spotted the woman.

That was when the complications began. . . .

3

He found the blonde standing near a clump of bushes about ten feet to the left of the Malibu. She was staring wide-eyed at what was left of the four men who had tried to abduct her. Her arms were wrapped tightly around her body as if fighting off a terrible chill. Moonlight cut through the bare branches overhead, illuminating the lovely face framed with silver blonde hair. The face was still stretched taut with fear. Bolan saw her lips drawn tight in a near hysterical grimace. She saw Bolan then, and her expression fluctuated between confusion and even more fear.

"It's all right," Bolan said quietly as he moved past her toward the carnage around the Malibu. "You're okay now."

It was not necessary to check the bodies of the four men who had waited for him in ambush. The rapidly spreading pools of blood on the moonlit pavement beneath them gave mute testimony to their fate. They would terrify no more women. They would kill no more men.

The corpse of their final victim, the man the blonde had been on her way to meet, was scrunched up on the floor of the back seat.

Bolan turned and approached the woman. She kept stepping back as he came toward her, until a tree stopped her.

"W-who are you?" she asked in a quavery whisper. "Did Eshan send you?"

"My name is Phoenix," said Bolan. His ears picked up the sound of rapidly approaching sirens from at least two directions on MacArthur. "We'd better get out of here. Or do you want to wait for the police?"

"No! Please. . . take me with you."

Bolan extended a hand. "Then come on. It's now or never. We have to move fast."

She accepted his hand. He was surprised to find that hers was warm and vibrant, despite all that had happened.

They started toward Bolan's Corvette. But they never reached it. They were halfway there when a sedan came wheeling in at doubletime and burned rubber into a sideways stop only inches behind the Malibu.

Bolan cursed silently as two more tough guys jumped out. One held a handgun. The other was armed with a Thompson.

Damn!

The boys in the Malibu must have been in radio contact with a backup team. And now here they were, on the kill.

Apparently they wanted the lady alive. The guy with the chopper began raising it at Bolan and opening his mouth to bark a command at his partner.

Bolan's Uzi barked instead, catching the man in a tight pattern in the upper chest area. The guy died on his feet, jerking around in a death dance—with a dead index finger squeezing back on the chopper's trigger.

Bolan saw it about to happen and pushed the woman roughly to the ground beneath him as the Thompson stuttered a short blast, sending a dozen or more rounds zinging into a wild semi-circle as the corpse holding the weapon stumbled and fell.

When the Thompson's angry chatter subsided, Bolan lifted his head to pinpoint the second guy. It wasn't hard, and there was nothing to worry about from that quarter.

Backup Number Two must have caught some of the chopper's errant rounds. He was on his back amid all the other bodies, only he wasn't lying still. He was groaning—a murky, bubbly sound—and arching and twisting in pain as if he had no backbone.

Bolan looked at the girl. "Get in the car," he said.

Then, shifting the Uzi to his left hand, he unleathered the Beretta and approached the wounded man.

The guy's hardware lay a few feet from his

right hand. He didn't seem to be aware of it, but Bolan took no chances. He kicked the weapon aside, then knelt down next to the dude.

The guy was in intense pain and must have known he was dying. His lips were flecked with red. His hands were pressed against his abdomen but did nothing to stem the flow of life fluids that bubbled out between the fingers. His breathing was shallow, ragged, and forced. He seemed unaware that Bolan was beside him.

"Who are you?" Bolan asked calmly. "Who sent you after that woman?"

The guy's eyes opened into tight slits. He was a tough one, all right. A young guy who must have still thought that there was some honor among thieves. He spoke through teeth clenched against the pain, and Bolan could tell it was torture for him. But he spoke.

"Bastard...goddamn bastard...I'm not t-telling you shit....Bastard...."

Bolan sighed. "Have it your way," he said quietly.

He squeezed the Beretta's trigger.

Bolan hurried back to the car, climbed in beside the woman, gunned the engine, and got the hell out of there, continuing on into the park, away from the bodies and the two cars and the approaching sirens.

After passing two more turnoffs, Bolan pulled a left and took them back to MacArthur, catching MacArthur west toward Persimmon Tree Road, back the way they had come, toward that walled estate in Potomac, where Eshan Nazarour was temporarily residing.

He finally took time to give the lady beside him a long, sideways appraisal. She was hugging her door, watching him warily. He could see in the passing streetlights that the frightened lines of her face had softened some, but not entirely.

"Where are we going?" she asked quietly, nervously.

Bolan had the impression that she knew damn well, but he said, "Back home. Back where you started from."

"Do we. . . have to?"

"No. This is a free country. I can drop you off anywhere along here, if you'd like."

She mulled that over for a moment. Then she shook her head. There was something helpless about her that made Bolan want to reach out and touch her. To comfort her. But he did not.

"No, that's all right," she said finally, in a weak voice that was almost like a little girl's. "It wouldn't do any good. I'll go with you."

"Who were those men?"

"I—I don't know. I. . . don't know."

"Okay, we'll let that one go. Who are you? What's your name?"

He was pretty sure he knew the answer to

that. He was remembering the first thing she'd said to him as he'd come in out of the darkness after killing all those men: "Did Eshan send you?"

"Don't you know?" she said, staring straight ahead through the windshield, not even looking at him. "My name is Carol Nazarour. I'm General Nazarour's wife."

"Who was that man you were meeting? The one they killed?"

"It doesn't matter," came the harsh reply. "None of it matters. None of it. . . ."

That was, quite obviously, all she intended to say for the duration.

Bolan did not insist. There are times to push and times to lay off. For right now, the lady needed her space to recover from all that had happened, all that she had been through. Mack Bolan allowed her that space.

Complications, sure.

A corrupt Iranian general marked for assassination and his beautiful American wife who was up to her lovely blonde head in kidnapping and sudden death.

It promised to be one *hell* of a mission. And only he, because it was a hit team loose in American streets, was truly qualified to handle it.

Great.

Goddamn great.

4

Mack Bolan had mixed feelings about Washington, D.C., and its environs, which included Potomac, Maryland. The area had about it a sense of oneness with history that Bolan had experienced in few other places in the world. You could *feel* the spiritual presence of the great men who had walked this ground and done great things. The Washington Monument. The Lincoln Memorial. The Tomb of the Unknown Soldier, where Bolan had meditated on several occasions long after the city around him slept. Yeah. To experience Washington was to experience the essence of American pride and patriotism. But there was another side of Washington that Bolan cared for not at all.

A beautiful city, sure. *If* you ignored the sprawling black ghetto that surrounded the capital of this land of plenty. And that's exactly what most people did. Washington is not so much people as a state of mind. The city's only real industry is government, which employs nearly a half-million civilian and military per-

sonnel: about forty percent of the area's work
force. And if it is a town of scenic parks and
classical architecture and monuments to a great
past, then it is also a city of lies and deceit and
too many factions trying to buy too many pieces
of democracy with a strictly what's-in-it-for-me
philosophy. A city where the tax dollar finances
wasteful bureaucratic nonsense, while the ghetto and the problems it represents only grow
larger, and the only things that go up are the
taxes and the bureaucrats' salaries.

Mack Bolan was not a cynic by any stretch of
the imagination. Rather, he was a realist. He
knew that many good men and women worked
hard, long hours in the nation's capital to make
this country a better place to live. But they stood
little chance of succeeding in any large sense.
They were outnumbered and outflanked by the
bureaucrats and their red tape and the many interests they fronted. Somehow the country func-
tioned, the democratic process worked, and
sometimes decency and what was right did win
out. But not nearly often enough.

Bolan stayed as far away as possible from the
fat-cat lawyer legislators and what they were trying to do to a great nation. Col. Phoenix was a
man of direct action surviving in a complicated
world. He did his part away from sticky-fingered
senators and silver-tongued diplomats. He cast
his vote in every election, and he hoped that

enough people who felt the way he did were doing likewise. In a democracy there is always hope. But he generally stayed away from Washington proper unless his work called him there.

It was calling now.

He sensed Carol Nazarour growing tense in the Corvette's bucket seat beside him as he steered off Persimmon Tree, onto the road that fronted the northern wall bordering General Nazarour's temporary home.

Nobody could have guessed what she had been through. Bolan realized that this was a strong woman sitting next to him. As strong as she was beautiful. Sure, he could see the strain she was under—the tightness around the eyes and mouth. But she was keeping a stiff upper lip, too, and he liked her for that.

There was no sign of the Datsun that the kidnappers had left behind. It had probably been driven off by one of the backup team.

Bolan braked to the shoulder and killed his lights at the spot where he had first seen the woman moving furtively along the wall only a scant twenty minutes earlier. He turned in his seat to study her.

"How did you get out from in there?" he asked, nodding toward the property. "It wasn't by the front gate. You looked like someone crashing out of prison."

"I was," the blonde replied softly. But she ignored his question.

"You didn't have to come back here with me," Bolan reminded her sharply.

The woman sighed. A defeated, beaten sound. "He would have found me," she said, looking out through the windshield at the wall. "I've tried running before. He's always found me and brought me back. Or had me brought back." She seemed to realize for the first time that Bolan had pulled the car over. "Why did you stop?" she asked, turning to eye him with a new curiosity.

There was much that Bolan wanted to ask this woman. But there was little time. Much as his heart went out to Carol Nazarour and all she had been through, Bolan's top priority tonight was to nullify the Iranian commando team led by Karim Yazid. Bolan would not forget Mrs. Nazarour or her obvious plight. He would do what he could for her, tonight and later. But only after the top priority had been dealt with. For now, he had been delayed long enough.

He leaned over and unlatched her door, pushing it open for her. "I'm letting you out so you can break back into prison. Good luck, and keep your head down."

She didn't budge. "Who are you? I thought you were one of Eshan's goons."

"That's an interesting word for your husband's business associates."

The blonde made an unladylike sound. "My husband's business associates are some of the lowest scum walking this earth. Sure, they all wear expensive suits and are chauffered around in limos, but they're the people who are robbing their own country blind."

"Oil?"

"Some of them."

"Mafia?"

Her feminine blue eyes were dagger points of ice. She considered that for a moment. Then she blinked and the spell was broken.

"Maybe. Listen, if you aren't one of my husband's goons, then who in hell are you?"

"You'll find out soon enough. Now get a move on, lady. We'll talk later."

She studied him for another moment, then reached over and touched his wrist with her fingertips. "Thank you for the ride, and for saving my life."

Then she was out of the car. The leather coat and bouncing head of blonde hair disappeared into the darkness.

Bolan slipped the car into gear and continued on toward the front gate of the grounds. The skin of his wrist seemed to tingle where Carol Nazarour had touched him.

A beauty.

A tragic beauty.

She had tossed in her thanks for saving her

life almost as an afterthought, as if she herself
had doubted whether that life was really worth
saving.

The main entrance to the grounds was set in the
northwestern corner of the wall. And the general *had* gone hard. Yes, indeed.

The wall itself was twenty feet high and three
feet thick. At first glance it appeared like that of
any of a number of similar walled properties
Bolan had noticed along the outer reaches of
Persimmon Tree. This was horse estate country.
The wealthy liked their privacy. But the aura of
respectability was dispelled when one reached
the front gate, which looked like nothing so
much as Leavenworth Prison. The entrance had
been designed to discourage the most determined gate crasher. The drive to the gateway
was angled so that no vehicle seeking forceful
entry could pick up enough speed to ram
through the gate or the reinforced fence. Entrance onto the property was not *gained*: it was
permitted. There were two brick guardhouses
situated one after another, at opposite sides. A
gate stretched across the entrance in front of
each gatehouse.

A cold-eyed guard checked Bolan's ID while
the man's twin stayed behind bulletproof glass,
cradling a Ruger Mini-14, little brother to
Bolan's M1. Guard Number Two never took his

eyes off Bolan while the other okayed the ID and moved to unlock the fence barring entrance to the narrow corridor.

The scene was repeated at Gatehouse Two.

Bolan was impressed with the general's security. Vehicles had to pass through a two-stage entrance, stopping and slowly negotiating the narrow corridor, which was barely wide enough to accommodate a standard American car.

There was a third backup guard at Gatehouse Two. And fifty feet beyond the checkpoint, snaking off in both directions in the darkness, stretched another chain-link fence laced with barbed wire, the upper four feet angled outward and probably electrified. Beyond the fence, the grounds of the estate extended in a rolling, gradual incline toward the house. The pebblestone driveway was about eighteen hundred yards long.

Bolan coasted toward the house in second gear. He was seeing and absorbing all he could that was relevant to the terrain where the coming battle would be fought.

Halfway to the house he passed another guard shack, this one discreetly nestled amid a dense cluster of dogwoods. But Bolan was not required to stop. Two guards were visible, and one of them waved the car by. The upgrade became more pronounced, and moments later, the driveway arced onto a sort of plateau and widened into a parking area.

Bolan parked amid a handful of darkened vehicles and unloaded his gear from the sports car.

An Olympic-sized swimming pool, empty now, and a cluster of cabanas separated the parking area from the house.

Bolan hurried along a stretch of cobblestone walkway that encircled the pool. The grounds were dark. Moments later the main house began taking shape in the moonlight.

The red brick structure was a two-story holdover from the nineteenth century. Dated, but with its elegance intact. Several of the windows were lighted.

A man stood in the open front doorway, waiting for Bolan. An Iranian, early forties, of rather slight build, whose outstanding feature was the set of deep worry lines that furrowed his face.

"Colonel Phoenix? We expected you some time ago. I just finished speaking with Mr. Brognola. I'd called to ask if you'd run into any delays."

"No more than usual," Bolan grunted, declining further explanation. He thought quickly of the background data that Aaron Kurtzman had supplied on the cassette regarding the general's group. "You must be Dr. Nazarour."

The Iranian nodded, visibly impressed. "I am Mehdi Nazarour. I serve as my brother's physician," he confirmed. He spoke with the perfect clipped cadence of a foreigner, but Bolan sensed a barely subdued nervousness about the man. The general's brother stepped aside, holding the door open for Bolan. "I will tell Eshan that you have arrived," he said as Bolan stepped into the front foyer.

The physician indicated a door across the hallway that led off the foyer. "Perhaps you would care to wait in the study. Mr. Rafsanjani is in there now—my brother's secretary and assistant. My brother will be only a few minutes, and I'm sure Mr. Rafsanjani will make you comfortable and fill you in on any details about our place here. As I say, we've been expecting you."

Then the front door was closed behind Bolan. The brother exited to another area of the house. There was a deathly stillness about this building. Bolan crossed to the study door. He could not ignore the feeling in his gut that he had just stepped into a nest of vipers.

The study was warm, comfortable, softly lighted, and lushly appointed. Two of the walls were lined with books, ceiling to floor. Another wall boasted a well-stocked bar and video setup. The wall behind the wide desk must have been a picture window. At the moment a curtain covered it, draped against the night.

A short, somewhat effeminate man of indeterminate middle age rose from behind the desk as Bolan entered and set his ordnance temporarily across the surface of the bar. The man reminded Bolan of Peter Lorre, the forties movie actor.

A smile seemed to slide onto the man's bland face. He leaned across the desk with arm extended as Bolan approached. His handshake was loose and cool. "Ah, Colonel Phoenix." The guy even had a high-register Lorre voice. "We had begun to worry about you. May I fix you a drink?"

"No, thank you."

"I am Abbas Rafsanjani," the man said with a slight bow. "It has been my privilege to serve General Nazarour both in Iran and in our travels. In our exile. I want you to know that I am at your disposal, Colonel. As are all the members of the security force outside."

"I appreciate that," Bolan said with a nod. He was trying to penetrate those poker eyes and coming up with zero. "What about the house staff? Cooks and such?"

"The entire house staff was dismissed at the close of yesterday's workday," said Rafsanjani. "As you may know, we had intended to be out of your country by this time. The staff has been reduced to the general's two personal bodyguards, myself, and of course the general's

brother and Mrs. Nazarour." At a sound from
the door, the aide looked past Bolan. "Here is
the general now."

Bolan turned to see the study door behind him
opened by a burly guy in a security guard uniform that matched the ones of the men outside.
The guy held the door open while another uni-
formed man wheeled in General Eshan Nazarour. The man in the wheelchair waved a curt
dismissal, and the bodyguards walked out.

The general swung his wheelchair around in a
decisive, abrupt swivel that brought him face to
waist with Bolan.

The man in the wheelchair was in mufti, but he
was military right down to the tips of the spit-
polished shoes on his artificial legs. He was considerably older than his brother, and his face was
strong. The general's hair, which was brushed
straight back, was bristly and streaked with iron
gray, and thinning at the top. Unlike his brother,
Eshan Nazarour had no worry lines to mar his
countenance. Here was a man, wheelchair-
bound or not, who took life by the throat; he
commanded his life and the lives of those about
him, and expected blind obedience. A savage.
Right. And the savage was lord of his jungle.

"Colonel Phoenix," he rasped without intro-
duction, "we will discuss your business here
later—perhaps. First, there is something else to
be dealt with."

"There is security to be dealt with," Bolan replied coldly. "You know what we're expecting here tonight, General. It's going to be one helluva ruckus. And it's going to happen any minute. I suggest that one of your men give me a tour of the house and grounds immediately. I want to have a closer look at your security. Then we'll talk."

Nazarour wore the frigid, adamant expression of a man whose authority is rarely questioned. "We will talk *now*, Colonel," he hissed. "I demand to know why you were delayed in getting here tonight. And I want to know why you thought you could smuggle my wife back onto these grounds without my being aware of it."

Rafsanjani seemed stunned.

It had, yeah, become a *very* complicated mission.

Very suddenly.

Very unexpectedly.

Very *definitely*.

5

As Stony Man Farm's liaison with the Pentagon, with CIA headquarters, and with the White House, Harold Brognola had done his share of worrying since Mack Bolan's "new war" had commenced three missions ago. There was no way around it. Worrying just had to be a way of life when yours was a desk job and it was your best buddy out there in the field taking on the hairiest missions anybody could throw at him.

This latest task, the one Brognola had dropped in Striker's lap before the guy's heels had even cooled from his last assignment, was no exception.

A crack paramilitary assassination team: that's what Striker was out there taking on tonight. These dudes who intended to hit Nazarour were the absolute best in the business. Their record was proof enough of that. They had traveled the globe, systematically terminating "with extreme prejudice" those who had been marked for death by Iran's kangeroo-styled "holy courts." And now they were re-

portedly here in Washington, in Bolan's back-
yard. No exotic locales this time. No jumping
on board a jet for some foreign trouble spot. It
was all going down less than one hundred miles
up the pike in sedate, upper-class Potomac.

Yet it could be the toughest mission of
Bolan's new career if this hit team was even half
as good as their record indicated, and Brognola
had to acknowledge inwardly, glumly, that they
were that good. Bolan was out there tonight—a
bone-weary man still drained from his previous
mission, which had concluded only hours ago—
and he was going up against a disciplined unit,
each man of which would be Bolan's equal in
combat training and skills.

Fourteen of the bastards! And they would *not*
be bone weary. Bet on that: they would not be
tired. They would be open for business. There
was no telling how or when they would strike.
Each previous hit had been different, under different circumstances, with no discernible M.O.

Yeah. Tonight Potomac would see one shit of
a firefight. Of that, Hal Brognola was certain.

Damn Nazarour! A good man was out there
risking his life because of that Iranian jackal.
How had Nazarour been allowed into the country in the first place? Or rather, whose palms
had been greased? When this thing was over and
he had a few spare seconds to breathe, Brognola
promised himself that he would find out. Sure,
there was a good reason for Striker to be out

there tonight. A damn good reason, the way things stood now. This hit team had to be stopped.

Brognola fired the cigar jutting from the corner of his mouth. He glanced at his watch. Ten-fifty-nine. The team was going to hit within the next seven and a half hours. Before dawn. That was the one thing the previous hits did have in common: Karim Yazid and his men preferred night work.

April walked into the room, interrupting Brognola's thoughts. She was carrying two cups of coffee.

She handed one to Hal. "Nothing new out of Tehran," she reported. "Except positive confirmation from an additional source that the attempt is scheduled for tonight. Yazid's team caught a flight to Paris out of Tehran yesterday morning, just as our first source reported."

Brognola grunted. "And at Paris they separated, picked up their phony IDs, and caught separate flights into the States, to rendezvous somewhere in the D.C. area.... It's easy to backtrack *after* the fact."

"You're really upset, Hal," April said. "What is it? Bad news?"

"I don't know." Hal was scowling at the phone in front of him. "I got a call from Abbas Rafsanjani ten minutes ago. As of then, Striker hadn't shown up at Potomac yet."

"He must've run into something between here

and there." April's voice was carefully emotionless, concealing the ache that had begun to gnaw at her.

"I hope it's some sort of a lead," said Brognola, not looking at April. "It can't be the enemy. Tehran has no pipeline into Stony Man. To waylay him, they'd have to know where Striker was coming from. They don't know that. And we didn't get the mission data ourselves until two hours ago."

"Mack's all right," said April quietly, firmly. "He'll be at Nazarour's shortly. Obviously something has slowed him up, and he hasn't been able to get through to us. It's when he *does* get there that the trouble starts." The pain was reasserting itself. The dull anxiety of not being able to help in any way.

"It's going to be tough," nodded Hal, looking at her directly now. "But they've all been tough, April, since the beginning. Even before you came aboard."

"I know. I know. I just hope and pray he's ready to take these people on. He must be exhausted from the ordeal with Toni...."

"I've had my mind on that," mused Brognola. "But let's look at the facts. He's equipped with his usual hardware, and it's never let him down yet." The fed's voice, slightly gravelly, was getting firmer and more confident as his enthusiasm mounted.

"He can do spectacular things with the Auto-Mag and the Brigadier. The Uzi, as far as I'm concerned, was invented for him. He's also carrying some flash and concussion rifle grenades, and I know he'll use them with considerable imagination.

"Hell, when my people at Justice were up against Mack, he scared them half to death regardless of his physical condition, regardless of how well he was armed. He can break a man's back with his bare hands, and he has done so.

"But Yazid's crew," he added, "God knows what they'll be carrying. AK-47s and AKMs probably. That's what the *Cherikhaye* have used in the past. Got them from Libya. They'll have been smuggled into this country months ago."

He tapped the desk top impatiently.

"Personally I hope these assassins are stuck with PPSH-41 submachine guns that Iran manufactured for Russia during World War Two. Not a very impressive 9mm weapon, and Iran has stacks of them."

Brognola was clutching at straws, partly to placate April's concern as they considered the conflict to come.

But that concern was only made the worse by Hal's talk of weapon smuggling. It was incredible to April that there were Americans who would willingly participate in the illegal importation of arms into the country, especially guns to be used against the security and stability of the state.

People involved in the international flow of weaponry were jackals. She had researched the stories of the past few years about disgruntled secret agents turning to the highest bidder. She knew that score. Certainly where Libya was involved, so was a whole network of Westerners who saw profit in chaos, and they were rapacious animals. They were also diseased with greed. They would be their own undoing. It was hardly worth pursuing them before they choked on their own poisons.

"Will they smuggle everything in? Ammunition, grenades, launchers?" she asked.

"There's no other way they can secure that stuff," Hal replied, in a ruminative mood again. "But I'm not going to worry about that part of it. The treachery of officials and merchants within the country will take another mission altogether.

"My chief concern is that Striker has sufficient back-up from the people already at Nazarour's place. God knows what sort of characters the general's got lined up there, but unless they are all one hundred percent behind our man, he could conceivably be overwhelmed by force of numbers.

"Nazarour's little army has got to stand behind Striker. Otherwise Yazid's mob has the advantage, even if Yazid comes rushing in with rusty old UAR Carl Gustavs stolen from the ruins of the last Mid-East war...." The weary man chuckled humorlessly at his own personal picture of Third World incompetence.

"You're tired," April said. "Take a break. I'll stand in for you."

Brognola turned in his chair to stare at the phone.

Waiting for it to ring, to tell him whether Bolan was at Potomac yet, to tell him that everything was on track.

No, he would not leave this desk, under any circumstances. There was a small window facing east over the desk. He would see the dawn, sitting here.

He would see Mack Bolan wind up another mission.

Or he would see Mack Bolan fail. And die. For such a thing could happen. This was Bolan's third mile and the numbers would always be getting chancier.

Memories of Washington's 14th Street bridge, the 737 in collision with it in the winter of 1982, the awful travesty of human destiny that plunged the airline passengers into the icy twilight waters of the Potomac, haunted Brognola as he thought of the locale of this latest mission, this new taunting of death.

There was a feeling in his gut that one of these

days, one of these missions, Mack was going to get really hurt. His star had shone lucky for a long time now, backed by Mack's extraordinary skills and by a courage that eliminated all fear of death, as if he was, in a way, dead already. But that star might dim at any time. It was as if he could follow Striker's story only with an increasing certainty that, soon, something was going to put out the light.

"Christ Almighty," blurted Hal, still glaring at the phone. "Let me be! I'll hold the fort."

April Rose's nerve snapped at the harshness of his tone. Her modellike poise seemed to disintegrate as she leaned toward Brognola's impassive face and said scornfully at him, "Stop acting like a fool, sir. You'll do yourself harm and you'll jeopardize Mack . . ."

"And you stop, Stony Man Two, right now," said Hal, each syllable like a gunshot. "You speak above your station."

"For heaven's sake—"

"Quiet! I am White House liaison on the Phoenix Project." His patience had gone. "Frankly I have been concerned for some time about the hazards involved in your emotions toward Colonel Phoenix, and you force me to raise the issue."

"Sir, in matters of the heart. . . ."

"The heart be *damned*! Listen to what I'm saying!" shouted Brognola. He didn't aim to hurt. His intention was to define and deploy. "It is you who are endangering our enterprise. Your feelings for Mack put the long-term outcome at risk for the sake of a short-term, panicky response."

April's eyes were misting. Her superior's commanding manner and sudden thrust of criticism had cornered her. But she was not fainthearted, ever. She was a veteran of the Justice Department's Sensitive Operations Group and she had been rated expert at rocketry systems skills, .38 revolver use, electronic surveillance. This statuesque beauty was no blushing flower. Her rebound strategy right now was a defense based on subtle but vigorous attack.

"You know you cannot question my integrity, Hal," she said, standing tall again. "I don't panic. If there is a problem in all this waiting—in this suspense—it is your own stubbornness. You're hard as stone, and you cannot hear the heartbeat."

"Meaning?"

"When was the last time you spent an evening with Margaret? When did you last see either Catherine or Michelle?"

A wry smile forced its way onto Brognola's lips. The mention of his wife, so dear to him, and his two grown daughters now had *him* at the disadvantage. He hadn't been home to share time with his wife for days and days, since well before Mack began mopping up in Minneapolis. His daughters, fine women both of them, one now in Ohio, the other married in New York, had by necessity become voices at the end of the telephone. Hal slowly rubbed his brow with a stubby hand.

"You think I'd be a more helpful person to us all if I put in an appearance at home occasionally, is that it?" he sighed.

"More or less," April replied, smiling slightly. "You do need a break, Hal. For the sake of your own family and for Stony Man."

"I'm thirty years older than you are, young lady. What do you know about an old man's needs? I never mention my family, they are my secret. But you're right. This tension is getting to me. We all need a support system. . . ."

He looked at her sheepishly, his eyes now twinkling with humor. "Will you forgive me for yelling at you, Miss Rose?"

"I cracked and I'm the one who's sorry," said April, turning slightly to face the wall covered in charts, a map of the world and a map of the U.S. "It's just that I can't bear it when Mack is at the mercy of those who aid and abet terrorism. I do have personal feelings for him, yes, and I have done ever since he saved my life in Tennessee."

Brognola nodded. It was an incredible time back then and he would never forget it. The episode April referred to was when the USJD had given Striker one week to hit six areas and finish off that particular bloody mile. In those days, of course, April was a fervent pacifist, and accepting an assignment as driver of the War Wagon was as aggressive as she would get. Until the Mob got its hands on her in Nashville and Bolan had to blaze his way to her rescue. Since then she had become a new woman.

"If there are people helping a hit team to operate in this country," she continued, "then I want us to take out those people now."

"Sure, April, I know," agreed Brognola, his respect for this strong woman confirmed by everything she said. "It's bad enough that we have a hit team in the country at all—definitely an event of the late seventies and eighties. It would have been unheard of at any other time. Makes me feel like an old man. . . .

"But the truth is, we don't have any information on who their accomplices are. Yet. I'm reasonably certain that there are no pro-Iranian gunrunners and arms dealers among the new amateurs at that business. I mean any of those out-of-work Special Forces vets hanging around for some action in Fayetteville or Hawaii. It's my opinion that the supply route is through a different sort of organization altogether."

"That's interesting," said April, her eyebrows raised in anticipation.

"I think the arms source has been too skillfully covert, too successful, for a bunch of embittered ex-soldiers moaning about social neglect. I believe we'll find some old friends from civilian life involved in this. I look forward to the unraveling of it."

"You mean the Mob, don't you?" April was barely able to conceal her pleasure at identifying the enemy. And it was an enemy already decimated by Mack, it just needed to be hacked back every now and again. Great. This would be an adversary he could get his teeth into, deep into the carotid artery once more. Things were looking up at last. Her body responded with exhilaration at the thought of it, extinguishing exhaustion.

"Hal," she said, picking up a wrapped stogie from the head fed's desk and handing it over to him in a celebratory gesture. "Have another cigar."

For the first time that night, Hal smiled with something approximating real delight. "I think I will," he said, grinding the dead butt of his previous one in the ashtray. "And yourself?"

"Thanks, but no," grinned April Rose. "I'm trying to give them up."

"Good for you," grunted Hal, enjoying himself for this fleeting moment. "Come on, let's get some more coffee and fill in the time with some calls of our own. I've got an idea a little detective work is required of us."

6

Bolan had known physical giants who had been weak and as easily intimidated as lambs. Now here was a guy in a wheelchair, whom Bolan sized up immediately as probably one of the strongest, toughest, craftiest men he had ever confronted.

Sure, Bolan had seen his kind before. A cannibal. Blood brother to the Mafia dons that Bolan had deceived during his previous "life." A guy whose driving wheel was the lust to exploit and gain for his own ends, no matter what the cost to others. That lust was fueled by a strength of will that would only be conquered by death.

And somehow General Nazarour knew that Bolan had brought Carol Nazarour back to the grounds.

How much else did he know? Bolan wondered.

Finally he responded to Nazarour's query regarding the general's wife.

"Why not ask the lady herself?" Bolan grunt-

ed. "I'm not here to play question and answer,
General. Nor to take orders. I'm here to protect
your ass until dawn." He glanced across the
room at the second Iranian. "Rafsanjani. I
want you to take me on a tour of the house, then
take me to your security chief."

Rafsanjani paused, looking at General Nazarour.

The general seemed to be considering something. Then he nodded and some of his coldness
thawed. He seemed to Bolan like a jungle
animal relaxing. But an animal of prey nonethe-
less.

"Forgive me, Colonel. Perhaps I was a bit
presumptuous. But I would ask you to consider
my situation and not 'stonewall' it, as you
Americans amusingly say. My life is at stake
here. You are a military man. I am a military
man. I observe signs of a struggle about the
knees of your slacks. I must know what I'm up
against. Have you engaged the enemy?"

Bolan changed tactics, too. It would do no
good to alienate Nazarour. The odds tonight
were already stacked.

"I engaged someone," Bolan nodded. "Some
men tried to abduct your wife. I intervened."

The general's face remained impassive.
"Were they Iranian?"

"Not that I could see. We shot it out over in
the Canal Park. I killed six of them."

Nazarour's eyes blazed. "You might have learned something from them," he snapped. "You could have questioned them."

"I had no choice. Any idea who they were?"

"None. Unless they were working in connection with this assassination team."

"That's not very likely," grunted Bolan. "From what I've heard, this team doesn't need any help. Now if you'll excuse me, General, I'll be about my business."

Rafsanjani stood by the door, holding it open for Bolan but with his eyes on Nazarour.

Nazarour read the unspoken question and nodded. "Show him everything he wishes to see," he instructed his aide. "And send my men in here."

"Yes, General."

Bolan stepped out into the corridor, and Rafsanjani followed, easing the study door shut behind him. Bolan glanced up and down the hallway. There was no sign of Carol Nazarour.

"How did the general know that Mrs. Nazarour and I came back together?" he asked the aide.

Rafsanjani's eyes were cold as polished marble. "The general is master of this house," he replied coolly. "My allegiance is to the general. I owe him my life. I would do anything for him." Here he paused for effect. "Please wait,

Colonel, while I see to the guards. Then we shall begin our tour.''

The old house was as much a museum as a residence. It had been modernized, of course, in all the necessary ways. But the renovation was so skillful and so complete that Bolan found Rafsanjani's tour of the premises to be almost like stepping into the past. Civil war decor graced one room, while another room was furnished in a turn-of-the-century motif. And above it all hovered emanations of still something else.

Something decadent.

Bolan and Rafsanjani were at the southwest corner of the house, checking the metal mesh that secured a pantry window, when Bolan gave voice to his thoughts.

"Tell me," he said conversationally, as he and the secretary were leaving the pantry toward the stairway to the second floor. "Do you ever pick up certain...certain vibes, living in this place?"

Rafsanjani permitted himself a thin-lipped smile. He seemed to see Bolan in a new light. "My respects, Colonel. You are a man attuned to the metaphysical planes of existence. There is indeed an...aura about this old house." The Iranian spoke almost reverently. "Perhaps it is the evil that the house has absorbed from its inhabitants over the past century."

"When was it built?"

"Some five years before your Civil War. In 1855. The general had me thoroughly research the title of the house when we moved here earlier this year. There is new money and there is old money in Potomac, or so I am told. This house goes very far back in time. Much has happened within its walls."

"Much that was evil?"

"The man who built the house was an arms manufacturer," said Rafsanjani. "A profiteer. He went on to make a fortune by selling his wares to both sides of that conflict. The building was renovated around the turn of the century by a gentleman who was adept in financial maneuverings in the areas of railroads, oil fields, and coal mines. A subsidiary corporation of a major oil company now holds the title. Yes, I would venture to say that *much* evil has transpired between these walls during this past century. Many souls have been bartered for."

"And your soul, Rafsanjani," Bolan said quietly, his eyes carefully scrutinizing everything as they walked, "what of it? Has it been sold to the devil?"

This brought only another thin-lipped smile. They had reached the second-floor foyer. The stairway had been widened to provide space for a motorized conveyor equipped to handle a wheelchair. Rafsanjani moved briskly toward a door at the head of the stairs, acting as if a brief metaphysical discourse had never occurred.

"This is the general's room," he announced as he opened the door and stood aside for Bolan to enter. "I would request that you give it an especially detailed examination...."

Bolan gave a thorough inspection to the general's bedroom. The window faced the front yard of the house. A skilled commando—as the men in Yazid's group undoubtedly were—would have no difficulty scaling the wall below the bedroom window and gaining access that way. There was no other means of outside entrance, and the general would be safe enough up here if there was a guard to protect the stairway and upper foyer—and the entire exterior.

It took Bolan and Rafsanjani only seventeen minutes to complete their security check of the house, but it was a thorough job. Bolan had inspected every room, every nook and cranny in that old pile of brick.

Except for one.

The door to Carol Nazarour's room was locked. No one responded to Rafsanjani's discreet but distinct rapping on the wood panel. And Rafsanjani claimed not to have a key.

"My orders are never to disturb Mrs. Nazarour unless it is under the most extreme conditions," the aide explained. They were waiting for a response that was not forthcoming.

"Have you seen her since she came back into the house?" asked Bolan.

"I have not."

"Has the general spoken with her?"

Rafsanjani's hooded eyes became wary. "I do not know. As I explained earlier, Colonel, my allegiance is to the general. This is purely a logistical alliance between you and us. Do not involve yourself in analyzing the relationships that confront you here, Colonel. We will separate in a few hours, never to see each other again. Mrs. Nazarour's room is identical to her husband's. That is all you need for our purposes tonight." He turned away from the door. "Let us continue...."

"Relax, buddy," Bolan replied. "If the lady needs privacy, that's all right with me. I'll be around if she wants to talk to me later." He made sure he was close to the door and speaking loudly.

A simple mission. Uh huh.

As he and Rafsanjani moved on to the next room, Bolan found himself formulating a theory about Carol Nazarour and those hoods who had tried to become kidnappers and ended up dead men in the C&O Canal Park—and about the man Nazarour's wife had been on her way to meet. The man Bolan had seen gunned down.

If Bolan's theory was correct, then Carol

Nazarour's intentions and allegiance would be a crucial factor in the general's safety tonight.

Bolan hoped like hell that the lady had been listening behind that bedroom door. That she would make contact with him.

The blonde was a beauty. Of that there was no doubt.

But Bolan wondered what *else* Carol Nazarour was.

Where would her allegiance rest when the coming battle was raging? Would she be friend?

Or foe?

He had doubts about her capacity for what might be called civilized behavior. She seemed to have bartered her integrity for a lousy price already. Though it was not yet possible to be sure of that.

But about the civilized behavior of the non-nationals in this place he had no doubts whatsoever. All politeness was show. Gentility was a sham. The true nature of these exiles was barbarous: for them, life was cheap—unless it was their own.

"Any other hidden access to the house?" Bolan asked Rafsanjani. "A bricked-up rear porch, or conservatory, greenhouse?"

"Ah, the greenhouse," said Rafsanjani, his face lighting up. "Acute of you to mention it." The little man raised a forefinger and shook it at Bolan in mock admonition. "That is my favorite adjunct to the house, my personal play space. Mine alone.

"I shall show it to you because it will give me pleasure. It is in fact attached to the building, but there is no way into the house from it. It is accessible only from the outside. Come."

The two men proceeded downstairs and out through the front door. Bolan maintained his appearance of alertness, though he was endeavoring to pace his energy for the crisis to come. His reserves were already sorely taxed.

Around the back of the building stood a small greenhouse with a roof that sloped against the wall of the house itself. It was lit from within.

As they entered it, Rafsanjani pointed to a wooden hutch on the outside of the door. "Rabbits," he said simply. "My idea."

Inside the greenhouse, the humidity gave forth a rank odor of unusual plant life. Bolan surveyed the structure swiftly. There was nothing of interest to him there.

"These are exotic herbs I am growing," said the Middle Easterner in his whining voice. He intended to capture the American's interest in an obscure hobby. "The protection of them is everything to me. They are my sole existing connection with the homeland, apart from the general, of course."

He waved his small hand in a gesture of territorial power, his plants tall but slightly bowed in the artificial atmosphere. "I would not advise entering farther than this point," he added.

"No?" queried Bolan. He was becoming aware of a sinister delight in this unpleasant little man's attitude.

"It would not harm you lethally, but it will kill all vermin of lesser scale." Rafsanjani pointed to the slanting roof. "The metal bar crossing the roof there—it is emitting a silent scream!"

His eyes were now blazing with intensity. He was looking at Bolan with the gaze of a mad scientist. These people gave the big guy the creeps; he was beginning to feel alien in his own land.

"You have a sonar device at danger pitch there? Why?" he rasped. He was going to cut through this crazed man's crap with brutal force if need be.

"To preserve and protect, of course," giggled the Iranian. "Watch."

He stepped out of the greenhouse to the rabbit hutch, opened the hutch door and, clutching the animal around the neck, pulled out a piebald rabbit from its bed of straw.

Before Bolan could stop him, Rafsanjani flung the creature through the air. As it traversed the space beneath the bar across the roof, suddenly the animal plummeted to the ground. It was screeching eerily as it lay spreadeagled on the dirt of the floor. Then two streams of blood poured from the helpless animal's ears, and its eyes all but popped from its head. A sickening twitch or two and then silence.

It had been struck stone-dead by the invisible force of sound. Bolan was speechless. The act was wanton and disgusting, the sight of it was an ugly, nauseating thing.

But Rafsanjani was thirsty for more.

"Again?" he squealed as he moved toward the cage.

"Enough," shouted Bolan. With the side of his hand he chopped at Rafsanjani's arm as it reached for the cage.

The act paralyzed the cruel man on the spot. Far from dropping from the blow, Rafsanjani's arm sprung back and stayed outstretched, stiff with shock, as his jaw dropped and he stared at the spreading welt with watering eyes.

"Damn you," he gasped, shaking his arm and dancing about like a struck ape.

"Damn *you*," spat Bolan. He had no patience with indiscriminate animal killers. Self-defense he applauded, some revenge he could condone, but the careless arrogance of super-predator Man sickened him with its spoiled, idle abuse of the lesser creatures. "You touch another animal in that cage and I'll jam your face into the back of your head."

He pushed Rafsanjani impatiently to one side, sending the dazed Iranian staggering along the pathway. He swung the wooden-framed wire door of the hutch wide open.

"I'm releasing these toys of yours," he said. "Better they face the danger of dogs and highways than your sick whims.

"They'll be a damn sight safer away from this place tonight anyway," he added. "You'll all be like scared rabbits when this invasion comes down. And frankly," he said, turning to offer Rafsanjani an open sneer, "I'm beginning to look forward to it."

7

The head honcho of the security force was a sur-
ly, heavyset dude named Minera. Bolan and a
chastened Rafsanjani found him in what had
once been the estate's stables. But no fine-
muscled racing champions were being bred here
now. The old wooden structure had been renovated to serve as the security force command
post.

Minera wore the same navy blue uniform as
the other guards. His right hand rested habitual-
ly on the butt of a Dirty Harry model .44 Magnum holstered at his hip.

When Rafsanjani informed Minera who
Bolan was and why he was there, the guy's response was an angry glare at the newcomer.
"Nobody told me there was gonna be help rung
in from the outside," he groused. "What's
wrong?" he demanded of the Iranian. "You
don't think me and my boys can handle this
tonight?"

"It's a matter of cooperation," Bolan inter-
jected coldly. "If you don't want to cooperate,

you can leave now and we'll carry on without you. If you're going to stay, I'll want a tour of the grounds. I'd like to personally inspect your security."

Minera backed down from the confrontation immediately. "I've got twelve men out there tonight," he said. "Besides the five at the front gate and the two in the guard shack on the driveway, I've got three more men out on foot patrol with dogs and the two inside the house with the general. They even watch him go to the bathroom."

"How are you set up electronically?"

"We've got rotating infrared cameras at all the corners of the outside wall." Minera touched the walkie-talkie at the hip opposite the .44. "Plus I'm in radio contact with my men at all times, and I've got a souped-up golf cart over there to get me anywhere I need to be fast."

Bolan started toward the golf cart.

"Let's take a ride," he suggested to Minera. As he and the security chief climbed aboard the nearby contraption, Bolan said to Rafsanjani, "Please return to the house and stay inside. Tell the others to do the same. I think Minera's men should be ordered to shoot on sight tonight. That means we have to restrict movement in the critical area, which in this case means the whole damn estate."

The Iranian again executed his slight bow.

"Whatever you think best, Colonel," he said in his Peter Lorre voice, then he turned and walked away.

"Never did care much for that weasel," Minera grunted to Bolan when Rafsanjani was out of earshot. He turned the ignition key and gunned the golf cart's engine to life. "Well, let's get this show on the road. We can start with a run along the inside perimeter and track down that dog patrol...."

The grounds of the estate had all the natural beauty that a man could ask for. The rolling hills were broken by clusters of dogwood and a lazy, meandering stream. But the natural beauty of the land was marred by the general's security modifications, especially the length of chain-link and barbed-wire fence that ran parallel to the brick wall. Pleasant geography or not, Bolan felt the same ugly emanations out here that he had felt cloaking the main house.

And he decided the security was not all it could be.

As he and Minera went bumping along in the powerful golf cart, Bolan put his thoughts into words. "Why no inner compound?" he asked the security honcho. "The house is on high ground, but it could be made safer."

"The general didn't think he was gonna be here this long," Minera explained. "Things got tied up."

"How long have you been with the general?"

"Since the time he went to ground here," said Minera. "Going on ten months."

"What do you think of him?"

Minera's response was a noncommittal shrug. "It's a job," he growled. That was all he had to say on the matter.

Bolan suggested that one man from the dog patrol be transferred to the first gatehouse at the front entrance. Minera went along with the suggestion, but the guy's surliness was never far from the surface.

Bolan left the security chief, who headed back to his post, and started walking a straight course up a rise toward the house, some two hundred yards away beyond a clump of trees.

Once he had topped the rise and disappeared from Minera's view, Bolan dodged off course and into the trees, out of view of anyone who might have been tracking his movements with night sight equipment. If pressed, he could always offer the call of nature as an excuse.

It was past time for contact with Stony Man Farm, and Bolan wished to make contact without any of the Nazarour household or staff knowing about it.

A lot more was wrong here than a busted marriage, and Bolan needed the full picture. For the time being, his strategy was to give these people free rein. To not let them know that he sensed something wrong with the picture here. He would give the principals of this drama a free rein, yeah. And they would show their true colors. And someone would then make a mistake.

That mistake, whatever it would be, could be Bolan's handle onto this thing.

He brought up the compact transceiver from under his jacket and depressed the transmitting button. The unit linked Bolan to Stony Man Farm via a government ultrahigh-frequency band expressly forbidden for public use. The transceiver was locked into a D.C.-area scrambler station, which gave the transmissions airtight security and additional range.

"Striker to Stony Man. Come in, Stony Man."

The transistorized crackle of April's response carried a brightness of profound relief.

"This is Stony Man, Striker. Go ahead. Are you all right? Over." Her voice was lively, but her questions were efficiently procedural.

"Alive and kicking," chuckled the big guy in black. "But this thing is twistier than it looked. I need some information."

"Name it, Striker. You should know that Hal and I are looking into some rough connections both sides have. We'll report soon. But go ahead."

"Run a check through police channels for

'anything you can get on a shooting at Canal Park,'' said Bolan. "It happened about a half-hour ago. I also need anything you can give me on a man named Minera. He's the security chief out here. I've got a hunch about this one. Check him out with the Org Crime Bureau downtown. I also need a license number IDed." And he recited the license number of the blue Datsun.

"Roger," April acknowledged crisply. Then a hint of something else crept into her voice. "Striker, what kind of shape are you in?"

Bolan's own voice softened. April was, yes, a most important person in this warrior's life. He had his close buddies in this cause—men like Brognola and Jack Grimaldi, who had made sacrifices that easily matched his own and who were united with him in this new cause—but April alone offered Mack Bolan the strength and friendship that these men did, plus the compassion, comfort, and understanding that can only be supplied by the female of the species.

"Don't worry about this guy," Bolan assured her. "Everything is running smoothly so far. Anything from the Potomac authorities?"

"They're operating full strength," April's voice replied, its cool professionalism once again intact. "They're patrolling for any unusual signs of activity, but nothing so far."

"It's a long shot anyway," Bolan said. "This hit team will outmatch any local suburban force, no matter how good the force is. Tell them not to engage Yazid's group if they do locate them. Just pinpoint them for us, if possible."

"Roger, Striker. We'll advise if they spot anything unusual heading your way."

"Now I'd better get back into the action around here before I'm missed," said Bolan. "Get that information together as quickly as possible, April. I'll make contact again in sixty minutes—unless things are popping. Over and out."

He deactivated the unit and replaced the transceiver at his belt. Then he left the trees and resumed his approach to the main house.

The place was as secure as possible, sure.

But something was wrong.

To Bolan, every one of the security guards had looked like nothing less than a transplanted Mafia street soldier. He knew the type by heart, and *these* were the type. And that went for Minera, too.

A nest of vipers, yeah.

Bolan knew that not all of his problems would be coming from beyond that wall tonight.

8

Nazarour's brother stood in the shadows of the house and watched the big American approach. Colonel Phoenix had materialized out of the darkness from the direction of the front gate and guardhouse. Dr. Mehdi Nazarour had never seen a human being move with such economy or such compatibility with his surroundings.

As the big American in black strode past him toward the front door, Medhi stepped from the shadows, speaking softly.

"Uh, Colonel. May I have a word with you?"

The American swung around, iced-over eyes scanning the darkness, making sure the speaker was alone.

His response came in the same low whisper.

"Hello again, Doctor. What can I do for you?"

"I must speak with you on a matter of utmost urgency, Colonel. Please. Step back here where we won't be seen."

Dr. Nazarour returned to where he had been standing, and the American accompanied him.

All the while it was obvious to Medhi that the big man was keeping his fingers only inches from the butt of the impressive weapon that rode low on his right hip.

"Yes, Doctor, what is it?"

Medhi Nazarour felt drops of perspiration beading along his forehead, in spite of the chill.

"I, uh, only wanted to say, Colonel, how much my brother and I appreciate you lending your time and expertise to insuring our protection."

"You could have told me that inside," replied the man in black. "You'd better get to the point, Doctor, before we're missed and people come looking for us."

"Yes. Yes, of course. I only wish to say that—well, that you have many enemies here this night. . . if you understand my meaning."

Medhi Nazarour inwardly cursed the shivers that were coursing through him, causing him such difficulty in speaking. But he could see that the real meaning of his words had gotten through. The American's eyes glinted with interest.

"You suspect there's a traitor among you?" asked the man called Phoenix. "Are you talking about your brother's wife and Rafsanjani? Or about Minera down at the gatehouse?"

Medhi felt his shivers intensifying. "Please. I

can say no more. But be warned. Expect trouble from any quarter."

He began edging away, anxious to end this confrontation. He was already wondering if he had made a terrible mistake.

"One moment, Doctor." Medhi felt himself frozen to the spot by the authority in the American's voice. "I'm glad I ran into you out here, away from the others. I'm curious. I haven't seen your brother's wife since I got here. Not even when Rafsanjani took me on a tour of the place. Where is she? Have you seen her?"

Medhi Nazarour wanted to hurry away, but instead he heard words escape his lips. "I was told by my brother that Carol had been through an unsettling experience. I was. . .instructed to administer a sedative."

"And did you?"

"Yes. She's asleep in her room."

"How long ago was this?"

"Shortly after you arrived. About forty-five minutes."

"How long does it take for the sedative to take effect?"

"Approximately fifteen minutes. It's a. . . very powerful sedative."

The American's eyes were now colder than before. So was his voice. "How was the sedative administered? What was Mrs. Nazarour's reaction to all this?"

"The sedative comes in tablet form. She

understood that it was her husband's implicit order that she take the tablets or face some sort of punishment. This has happened in the past. Rafsanjani has had to... to deal with her several times. Tonight he locked her into her room after I had given her the sedative."

"Locks? Punishments? That sounds more like a living hell than a marriage, Doctor."

Medhi's mind was screaming to him, *You must go! Be gone!* He began moving backward again, melting in deeper with the shadows, away from this American giant and his fierce glare, back toward the side door by which he had silently left the house.

"Please, Colonel. I must return before I'm missed. I simply wanted to warn you."

"Then one last question, Doctor. Why are you telling me these things? What is your motivation in this?"

It was the question Medhi Nazarour had dreaded hearing. It would be foolish to tell him too much. It could be a fatal error.

"I... must do as my brother says."

The words came to Medhi as if spoken by another. He barely recognized his own voice; it sounded weak and afraid. But the big American made no attempt to stop him or question him further, and before he knew it, Medhi was back inside the house and moving on soundless feet toward the back stairway that led upstairs to his room.

Medhi Nazarour detested himself and his weakness. He detested his love and physical addiction for the little packet of heroin that awaited him, hidden in his room.

But he needed the blissful release that the drug provided. It was his only escape from the horror that had become his life during these past two years of exile with his brother.

Medhi had been able to handle his addiction back in the days before the revolution in Iran. That was when he had been a successful physician appointed to the Shah's personal court. But now his entire existence revolved around that little packet of white powder and the bliss that was his at the stab of a syringe.

As a doctor in Iran, it had been possible for him to dose himself with small amounts of the purest heroin from his own practice. But here in the United States, he had no access to pharmaceutical narcotics, and was at the mercy of his brother, Eshan, who had become his sole supplier of the powder since they had fled Iran. Eshan had American connections that Medhi knew nothing about. These connections furnished Eshan with the drugs that his brother craved. Medhi's addiction had increased dramatically as the quality of what he injected into himself decreased, and he was forced to take more and more.

The doctor reached his room, padlocked the

door behind him, and went directly to where he had hidden his kit.

He had done what needed doing.

Now he could step out of this horror.

He began preparing his fix, heating the spoonful of white powder over the candle flame, the syringe held at the ready.

The horror was for men with the strength to face it. Men like his brother, Eshan. And the big American fighting man, Colonel Phoenix. It was *their* horror now.

Medhi's only real concern, which he also wanted to escape thinking about, was that Eshan's safety be insured. Medhi could not bear to think of facing reality without heroin. And by warning the American as he had, Medhi was sure that he had helped ensure the odds for his and Eshan's survival. And poor Carol's.

Medhi Nazarour held a firm, instinctive conviction that the fate of all of them rested in the hands of the big American.

Whoever he was.

9

Mack Bolan turned away from the confrontation with Medhi Nazarour with several answers to the puzzle that was tonight's mission.

He now knew, for instance, that the reason Carol Nazarour had not responded to his knock at her door when he had been on his security tour with Rafsanjani was that her husband had ordered her heavily sedated, and Rafsanjani had locked her in her room as an added precaution.

Yeah. A great marriage.

And Bolan knew Medhi Nazarour's motive in coming to Bolan, even if the good doctor had evaded the issue.

Dr. Nazarour was a junkie. Bolan had seen enough of the type in his two bloody miles through the Mafia hellgrounds. The eyes, the body language, a doctor who sweats at night—the guy was a walking advertisement for stiffer drug controls.

The trouble was, for every answer, more questions seemed to pop up behind it.

Like what exactly had Dr. Nazarour been

warning him against? Who was it who was working with Yazid's hit squad from the inside?

In this short hiatus before the bloody storm, Bolan could not ignore the other questions screaming for answers. It was time for another talk with General Nazarour himself. It was eyeball-to-eyeball, lay-the-cards-on-the-table time. Bolan stepped up his pace toward the front entrance to the house.

He had taken four steps when the small object landed at his feet.

He halted, crouched, reached for the Auto-Mag rather than the Beretta. Then a closer inspection revealed that this was not danger.

The object was a woman's low-heeled shoe with a folded piece of paper tucked inside.

Bolan retrieved the shoe, and faded back against the deeper shadows close to the house. The paper was white stationery; Bolan detected a faint whiff of exotic perfume on the night air as he unfolded it. He read the note, obviously written in hurried feminine script:

In back of house right now. Please. Tell no one. C.N.

Bolan tossed the shoe behind a thicket, pocketed the note, and moved cautiously around toward the back of the building. He unleathered Big Thunder.

So Carol Nazarour, if the note was to be believed, had not taken the sedative as ordered by her husband.

Bolan smiled to himself in the darkness.

Yeah.

He'd had the lady pegged as a special kind of woman, and she was proving him right.

He found her waiting for him under an ancient tree beside the rear of the house. She looked like a pretty college student. Jeans, the same leather jacket as before, and a canvas backpack slung over her shoulder. Her perfectly sculpted face beneath that breathtaking head of hair was taut with anxiety.

Bolan holstered the .44 and approached her, touching her lightly on the arm for obviously needed reassurance. He nodded at the backpack. "Running away from home, Carol?"

"Please. I'm an American citizen. I want to get out of here." Her voice was a desperate plea. A visible shiver coursed through her. "I don't want to leave the country with...these people."

Bolan recalled the shivering fear of Medhi Nazarour only moments before. "Life with the general must be a real bowl of cherries," he grunted.

"It's worse than you could imagine," she told him bluntly. "I stopped trying to run away after the first year. He usually sent Rafsanjani after me. Once they tracked me across Europe. I thought I'd got away. Rafsanjani waited until I was in line at the Frankfurt airport. After he had me alone, he had me. . .beaten. But always with leather gloves so there were few marks or bruises."

Bolan felt a red-hot rage building deep in his gut. "Why didn't you take off earlier tonight when I gave you the chance?"

"Because I thought you were one of them! Rafsanjani did that to me one time. He offered me a chance to leave. When I started to leave, he said it was only a test. And I had failed. So I was beaten again."

"But now you know that I'm not one of them, is that it?"

"Yes. Medhi, the general's brother, told me who you are and why you're here."

"I met Dr. Nazarour."

"He's the only one I can even halfway trust around here," said the blonde. "I feel sorry for Medhi, but I don't always trust him. He's a slave to his brother. He'll do whatever the general tells him."

Bolan was working at cooling the burning anger that was ripping at his insides. Rage would do him no good when the fighting began. It would only get him killed.

"How did you fall in with these creeps?"

"I was an army brat," she said simply. "And

a rebellious one at that. A real terror. A real ignorant little jerk who was too stupid to trust the wisdom of her parents. Dad was stationed with the NATO forces in Turkey. So was Eshan.

"I didn't fall in love with Eshan so much as I fell in love with his image. He wasn't in a wheelchair then, of course. That happened during the revolution, just before we had to flee the country. Before we started this life on the run.

"But when I met Eshan in Turkey, he was tall, dark, dashing, and mysterious. My parents objected furiously, but I guess I was also in love with the idea of one final rebellious gesture to let them know that I didn't need their guidance. That I knew exactly what I was doing." She shook her head and looked down at the ground, laughing softly without humor. It was the sound of irony. "If only they could see me now. But they're dead. They died in an automobile accident six months after I left home."

Bolan's senses were finely tuned to the immediate surroundings, but he heard no sounds of anyone in the area. Time was running out. The numbers were falling away.

"Who was the man you met outside the wall this evening?" asked Bolan. "The one who was killed."

"That was Tony. He was one of the men on the guard crew. But he didn't seem like the others. He could be. . . kind when he wanted to."

"Were you in love with him?"

She looked squarely up at Bolan. There was a bitter twist to her mouth. "Love? I don't think I remember what that word means anymore, Colonel. Tony was just someone to pass away the time with, when I needed someone to be kind."

"Was Tony going to take you away from your husband?"

"No. Tony was too weak to go against the men he worked for. And I think they discovered our relationship anyway. Or my husband did. My husband sent those men tonight, Colonel. They killed Tony and they were going to 'punish' me for my indiscretion, no doubt. Until you came along."

"And all on the last night that you were in the country," Bolan muttered. "Your husband has a flare for the dramatic. How did you get outside the wall?"

"I *thought* that I'd found a hidden tunnel. I discovered it one afternoon when I was exploring the house. I used it often to meet Tony. The tunnel looks as if it hasn't been used in a hundred years. But if Eshan had those men waiting to jump us when I met Tony tonight, then he must know all about the tunnel and everything else."

Again he nodded at her backpack. "And now you want me to help you run away, is that it?"

Her eyes pleaded desperately with him. An edge of panic slipped into her voice as she sensed his hesitancy. "Please, Colonel. I'm an American citizen, and you're an agent of this government. *Please* get me away from here! I don't want to leave the country with these people. I need your help."

"And you'll have it," Bolan assured her. "But I can't help you now, Carol. I'm here on a specific mission, and I've got to commit myself to that first.

"I'll see that your rights aren't violated further. But I'm needed here right now. I can't leave to accompany you somewhere else. I'll take you with me when I leave. That's the best I can do."

She glided close to him as he said that, molding herself to him until he could feel every warm, feminine curve of her body pressing against him. There was a subtle erotic fragrance to her blonde hair, which he recognized from her stationery. She entwined the fingers of her right hand through his and moved the palm of his hand upward across her leather coat, squeezing the hand fiercely when it was over her left breast. Bolan could feel the warmth of her even through the layers of clothing.

"Please," she whispered in a husky voice near his ear. "Get me out of here and I'll do *anything* you ask...."

But he already had her by the arms and was pushing her back.

"You've been around people too long who think sex is for power," he growled sternly. "I said I'd take you with me when I leave, Carol. But the mission comes first. There are no ways around that." He dropped his hold on her arms, and the icy blue eyes warmed a little. So did the voice. "Now get back to your room and don't budge. Wait until I come for you."

There was a pause. Then she seemed to accept that. She eyed him with the trace of a smile.

"You sound very confident, Colonel."

"It helps. You should try it yourself."

"You're right. I have been around creeps for too long. I forgot that there were men. . .like you. But what if you don't come back?"

Bolan did a quick weighing of priorities. The lady was an unknown factor, sure. But only in what she might do, not in the awful situation in which she was trapped.

He reached under his jacket and unleathered the Beretta Belle. "Take this," he said, handing it to her. "But use it with extreme discretion, Carol. A gun can get you into as much trouble as it can get you out of." He took another ten seconds to explain the basics of firing the weapon. "Can you handle it?" he asked as she took the weapon and slipped it into her backpack.

"I can handle it, Colonel," she said softly.

She leaned forward on her tiptoes one more time and planted a warm, moist but very chaste kiss on his right cheek. Then she spun around and was gone.

Bolan stared off into the darkness even after that damn fine set of curves had disappeared from sight. There are some women on this planet capable of getting that reaction from a man, and Carol Nazarour had the ability in spades. The exotic, erotic fragrance of her perfume swirled on the air in her wake, tantalizing Bolan's senses like the vague memories of a half-forgotten dream.

Some lady, yeah.

10

No one tried to stop Bolan as he passed through the front entrance of the house and crossed the hallway to the study door. The two security guards were stationed just outside the study, so Bolan knew exactly where to find General Nazarour.

The guards tensed and started to rise, hands reaching for their side arms, but they relaxed when they eyeballed the formidable figure of Colonel Phoenix. They let him pass.

Bolan entered the study without knocking. His eyes made a quick sweep of the room.

General Nazarour was seated in his wheelchair behind his desk.

Abbas Rafsanjani, looking more like Peter Lorre than ever, had been in earnest conversation with the general. Rafsanjani shot a cautious, conspiratorial glance over his shoulder toward Bolan, who was standing in the doorway.

Nazarour was first to speak.

"Come in, Colonel," he invited dryly. "You

have about you the air of a man who has something on his mind and needs to say it.''

Bolan heeled the door shut behind him without taking his eyes off either man.

''Your security looks good, General. But a few other things have changed.''

''What impertinence,'' Rafsanjani rasped under his breath. ''You, Colonel, are in severe need of some lessons in protocol.''

''I'll take them on my own time,'' Bolan barked. He glared at Nazarour. ''I need to speak with you, General. Alone.''

The general acquiesced with a nod to his aide. ''You may leave us now, Abbas. I'm sure I'll be quite safe alone with Colonel Phoenix.'' The general didn't take his eyes off Bolan as the eyes narrowed. He added pointedly, ''Only please tell the guards to listen closely for any...unusual sounds. Just in case.''

''But I do not understand your asking me to leave,'' Rafsanjani announced in injured tones.

''Yours is not to think or understand,'' Nazarour snapped sternly. ''Yours is to obey. Now be gone.''

The aide had no recourse but to depart. He stared darkly at Bolan as he passed.

When the study door had closed behind Rafsanjani, Bolan said, ''I've put a few things together, General. I know who those men were who tried to kidnap your wife tonight. They were sent by *you*, weren't they?

"You discovered that your wife was having an affair, and you sent some hired muscle around to make things tough on her for a while and teach her one of your 'lessons.'"

"Who have you been speaking to?" Nazarour demanded icily.

Bolan ignored the interruption. "Those men I blew away tonight by the C&O Canal were probably another shift from your own security force. Some of Minera's boys, doing a little moonlighting on one of their own and the boss's wife. You were paying them. And they were shooting at me. That is what's got me real mad at the moment, General."

The man in the wheelchair didn't flinch.

"You will kindly refrain from this discussion immediately, Colonel. My marital affairs are none of your concern. You will cease diverting energies from your given task."

"Your marital status is one of the things that has changed," said Bolan. "When you climb on board that jet tomorrow morning in Rockville— if you survive to board it—your wife will not be leaving with you. She's staying here in America. She's asked me to back her up on this, and I will."

Nazarour's swarthy expression darkened ominously. "Then it must have been my dear wife herself with whom you spoke."

"Don't worry yourself about the details," Bolan told him. "And if anything—*anything*—

happens to that lady, General, you will answer directly to me. Do you understand?"

Bolan didn't know what kind of response to expect. But he was surprised anyway.

Nazarour hardly seemed to consider the matter.

He nodded and waved a hand almost absently. "Fair enough. There are many fish in the sea, my good Colonel, as one of your American songs once proclaimed so eloquently. If the plaything wishes to be played with no more, she is free to go."

"That's real fine of you," growled Bolan with no attempt to hide the sarcasm. "And while we're so chummy with each other, there's another matter that needs to be dealt with."

Nazarour looked at him long and hard. He knew that the American had divined the one weak link in the chain that surrounded and protected this exile of his. It was a weak link invisible to the eye, but it resounded in the mind.

"My compliments, Colonel. Let me anticipate this matter that you speak of. It does credit to your powers of analysis.

"You are concerned as to how Khomeini's hoodlums have located me here at all, is that it?"

"Exactly," responded Bolan, laying down the ordnance he carried on the bar in the corner of the general's study; it clattered on the polished surface. "You have remained successfully undercover for the past nine months. So why the attack now?"

The crippled exile stared gloomily out of the window into the darkness. "It is a strange thing about my country," he said. "Iran is in the throes of a revolution, and Khomeini's high virtue and heartless terror reign hand in hand in the union of moral absolutism. And yet there is treachery everywhere, despite this terrible unison.

"It is not only outcasts like me who must fear disloyalty. Over one thousand of Khomeini's own imams have been assassinated in recent months. One thousand!

"However much one would like to believe that these killings are some sort of American revenge for the hostages—" and here Nazarour glared at Bolan, who was quietly observing the general as he expounded on his twisted world "—the fact is Khomeini has seen fit to execute twenty-five hundred of his own people in retaliation. So he must believe in the enemy within.

"And so do I. I believe I face an enemy within.

"Is it coincidence that I am to be a target tonight, on my last night in your country? Your Mr. Brognola informs me only a few hours ago that a murder squad has located me. How can it have done this?

"In the hours since, I have given it some thought, I can assure you. And so have you. But I know certain facts. I know that I have nothing to do with Iran's real enemies. I sincerely doubt that I am a victim of Tehran's secret intelligence. I am not worth it to them.

"The real enemies are the young people of what is called the People's Mujadeen. They are well-educated Islamics who think Marxism. This has nothing to do with me. I am not and never have been a socialist."

"Excuse me, General," interrupted Bolan, "But I believe Khomeini's enemies are also those who stole money from the country. Are you not the target of the Ayatollah's revenge because you systematically ripped off your own nation. . .?"

"Bah!" stormed Nazarour, banging his fist on the arm of his wheelchair. "That is bullshit, Colonel, if you'll permit me my favorite American expression.

"Iran can survive any number of capitalists, as it has in the past. My country has certain strengths, you know. It may puzzle you as to how Iran has survived the murderous regime of the Ayatollah.

"I will tell you how. It is in the ingenuity of the peasants, the slum dwellers of South Teheran and the folk of the rural areas. Their strengths once outsmarted the Shah's businessmen, and these strengths continue to overcome the privations of the strife and the embargoes of today.

"Persia is historically a land of thousands of tiny workshops that improvise brilliantly the production of otherwise unavailable spare parts. It is also a land of smugglers. That is how it is done. People like myself are not a central threat to Iran's destiny."

The general paused. His grim face suggested a measure of wisdom, despite its dissolute features. Bolan knew there was truth to what he was saying, knowledge born of the observation of history.

"No," continued Nazarour, "I am not the victim of Iranian spies. I am the victim of someone around me here, someone who wants me dead. My enemy is within my own security...."

Suddenly there were sounds from beyond the study windows, outside in the night.

Dangerous sounds.

Shouts, then the rattle of automatic weapon fire.

The report of answering fire.

More shouting.

Bolan swung toward the bar, regaining his weaponry. "So much for Persian destiny," he muttered. "We'll have to continue our conversation later, General. In the meantime, I would advise holding hands with those two bruisers outside."

"It is happening so soon?" Nazarour's knuckles were white as he clutched the sides of his wheelchair.

"Maybe they're shooting rabbits," grunted the big guy as he slung the strap of the Uzi over his shoulder, ensuring that the gun would ride in the small of his back. He belted up with his collection of garrotes and other silent killing instruments, plus the custom-made British Special Service style flash and concussion rifle grenades.

"I guess you might all kill each other this night," he added. "And I'm in the goddamned middle. That is the special ferocity factor of this new war," he muttered to himself. But he was keen to begin.

He next unzipped the leather carrying case, hoisting and rapidly checking the action on the M1. The impressive weapon sported the Smith & Wesson Startron passive infrared night sight. The Startron magnified what little light there was, so that a warrior could easily pinpoint his position in combat in relation to anyone using an active night spot. The Startron/M1 combo would serve well tonight. The M1 fired 150-grain .30-caliber ammunition and threw it hard and fast, so that a 600- to 800-yard first round kill was not only possible but probable. Bolan always preferred accuracy—one round, one kill—as opposed to spraying bullets all over the place. In addition to an automatic mode that enabled him to fire short bursts if necessary, the M1 was equipped with a rifle grenade attachment.

With the .44 AutoMag riding at his right hip, the big warrior was ready for extreme action. And he had armed himself fully in less than twenty seconds.

Bolan *had* to move fast.

He must meet the assault head on, with full fury.

He didn't waste time with any parting comment to the general. He hit the light switch, plunging the room into darkness, and stepped out into the hallway.

The guards were up, their guns were out, but they seemed instinctively to eye Bolan for instructions. His orders were curt and sharp: kill all the house lights, get everyone in the main group accounted for, and sit on them.

The guards obeyed with alacrity.

So much for preparations.

There was more firing from outside and the sound of a small engine being gunned to its max, approaching the house.

The numbers were completely gone now.

The attack was on.

Bolan left the house to engage the enemy.

11

The small engine being gunned that Bolan had heard from inside was that of Minera's souped-up golf cart. The small contraption came flying full speed around the darkened Olympic-size swimming pool and shuddered to a wild fishtailing stop on the cobblestone walk near Bolan, who had hurried down the front steps to meet Minera.

The security honcho's surliness had disappeared. His eyes were bugged out. There was a sliver of blood along his right cheek. Bolan could see that the back of the cart was riddled with bullet holes.

The head cock leaped from the cart, holding his Dirty Harry .44 and eyeing Bolan with profound relief.

"Am I glad to see you! All hell's broke loose!"

The guy was close to losing it. Bolan spoke to calm him, quietly yet forcefully.

"You're throwing a party and not inviting me? What happened?"

"Damned if I know," Minera grunted, making an attempt to pull himself together. "I was out checking on the dog patrol. On my way back in, I couldn't see anybody moving around in Gatehouse Two. I was gonna pull in and take a look, but I never got that far. Some guys were already coming around from the front gate on foot.

"We saw each other at the same time, and they opened fire. I got a few rounds off, then got the hell out of there to find you. I don't know what the hell went down out front, but I'd say we've been invaded!"

"What about the guardhouse on the driveway?" Bolan snapped.

He had already set out at a stiff jog away from the golf cart, along the cobblestone walk that ran the circumference of the pool, heading toward the front grounds.

Minera stayed with him, trying to catch his breath.

"The boys in the guardhouse have a light machine gun," he told Bolan. "They should be able to hold 'em for a while."

The sound of a chattering chopper drifted in on the night air, as if on cue, from the direction of the guardhouse, a distinct nine hundred yards down the driveway from where they stood.

Bolan and Minera had come to the far edge of the pool, away from the house.

"We split up one hundred yards short of the guardhouse," said Bolan. "We'll close in on both their flanks. You take the left; I'll take the right. Let's just hope your boys with the chopper keep 'em pinned down and busy."

Minera seemed more than happy to let Bolan assume command.

"Just don't expect too much from me, partner." The guard boss tossed a nod at Bolan's weaponry. "Looks like you came prepared. All my heavy hardware is back at the goddamn command post—*holy shit*! What's that?"

Minera stopped and pointed at a dark human form that lay sprawled out on the ground alongside the cobblestone walk.

Bolan broke stride and stepped over to the form, the M1 held ready for business. With one foot he nudged the body over onto its back.

It was no trap.

The dead man was Dr. Medhi Nazarour.

Someone had rammed a stiletto into the physician's chest just above his heart. The blade had gone in to the hilt.

Bolan stooped down and made a positive verification. The general's brother was dead, all right. Blood still oozed from the wound.

A fresh kill.

Bolan rose from examining the body.

"It doesn't play," he murmured, almost to himself. "They couldn't have made it in this far from the gate already. Not without us seeing them.''

Minera couldn't seem to pull his eyes from the corpse. "If it wasn't the attackers, then who—''

But Bolan had already started away from the body, continuing on his way in the darkness toward the fighting. The chopper was still yammering from the guardhouse down the road, its chattering sound punctuated by the popping of rifles and another handgun in the open air.

The guardhouse was holding its own, but Bolan could tell they were outnumbered. It would only be a matter of time. Unless he and Minera got there first to even things out.

Minera was at his side again, keeping stride. Bolan studied the guy from the corner of his eye as they trotted along together, heading away from the pool, traveling parallel to the opposite sides of the winding driveway.

Bolan knew that he and Minera had probably been on different sides of the fence in that last war of the Executioner's. That was against the Mafia. But that was then. This was now. Now Minera was an ally. Crazy, sure. Another twist in Bolan's life, thanks to the capricious whims of the jungle.

But Minera would be a good fighter in this battle if he was fighting for his survival, as indeed he was. Because Bolan had encountered no more formidable foe than the American Mafia, he knew now that at least he was sided with a man on whose fighting ability he could rely. Minera had lost the shakes he'd had when he'd first zoomed in on Bolan in that damned golf cart of his. The heavyset security chief even looked eager to get into the fray.

Both men were now jogging at full stride.

When it happened.

And Bolan knew they were too late.

The night air erupted with the hellfire roar of what sounded to him like a Russian-made RPG-7, and a fractured second later the guardhouse went up with an explosion of destructive flame and a thunderclap that lifted the roof off the building and blew out the windows, scattering glass and wood and human bodies into the night air.

The cloud of smoke drifting away on the breeze from farther down the driveway confirmed Bolan's guess. Only an RPG-7 smokes off a cloud like that.

The guardhouse blast echoed around the walls of the estate, then died away.

Silence.

Death stalked the hills and valleys of that walled-in hellground, and both Bolan and Minera knew it.

"Now what?" Minera growled in a low whisper.

"Get down," said Bolan. "Let me see what we're up against."

The question of what had happened to Medhi, the general's brother, would have to wait.

As Minera crouched low beside him, Bolan dropped to one knee and lifted the M1 to sight through the infrared scope. The Startron swept the acreage that undulated away from Bolan from this point.

At first he saw nothing. Whether the terrorist team had killed the general's brother back there by the pool or not, there was still no telling how fast the team commander would deploy his forces once they had gained entry past the front gatehouse and secured their escape route—*or* how long it would take for the individual teams to box in the house. They could already be splitting up as they advanced past the destroyed guard shack, to hit the house from different angles.

The Startron picked up three figures spread out and advancing cautiously along the left side of the pebbled driveway. Across the road, spread out in similar fashion as they approached, were another three men. And a point squad of four more were across the driveway, advancing past what was left of the guardhouse, without a moment's glance.

Bolan eyeballed AKS sniper rifles in the hands of the two flank squads. Two of the point men toted AK-47s; the other two hauled the rocket launcher gear. Ten men all told, advancing slowly but steadily in silence, never bunching together, never allowing one man to advance without a covering stance from other members of the team.

According to Brognola, there were supposed to be fourteen.

Bolan scanned upfield away from the right flank. In the greenish tint of the Startron's magnified light, he spotted more movement.

Minera's three-man cog patrol was hauling ass full tilt in from the outer environs, where they must have been patrolling when the assault had begun.

Bolan scanned back to the road. Minera's three-man patrol was approaching the Iranians on a direct collision course. But they couldn't know that. It was a heavy mismatch, with the outcome all too predictable. Those guys would die without knowing what had hit them. The Bolan response to that situation was characteristic of the man and without hesitation.

"Let's go," he grunted to Minera.

Minera was pretty sharp himself. He caught the play immediately and responded unquestioningly to Bolan's lead. The two set off at combat-quick pace along the drive, one to either side at about a 20-foot separation, advancing upon the invaders' rear. The security patrol was about a hundred yards out and closing fast.

With a bit of luck, the defenders could engineer a deadly cross-fire, which would make the contest a bit less predictable. But that was just a hope at the moment. In a firefight, anything could happen. As Bolan closed on this hot encounter, he experienced a brief flashback to another time and another war...and understood immediately why he had preferred to operate alone ever since. The unpredictability factor in combat increased geometrically with the numbers on each side. Bolan could think only for himself.

God alone knew how Minera's ragtag troops would conduct themselves in an encounter with a crack combat team. Or, for that matter, how Minera himself would react.

Bolan knew only that he would have the answer within a matter of heartbeats.

The moon was hiding behind scudding clouds, alternately lighting the scene with pale illumination just long enough to provide quick fixes on the developing scenario. The ten- man combat team was advancing slowly but purposefully across the darkened grounds, closing in on the house. They appeared to be formed into three-man squads with a point man leading a squad directly to his rear by about twenty paces, flanking squads to right and left twenty paces over, and another twenty to the rear in a wedge formation. These guys knew what they were doing. Which made the task more difficult for Bolan but certainly not impossible. He was getting cooperation from heaven...via those blessed little clouds that kept moving across the moon.

He had a quick, whispered conference with Minera, then went directly to work. The point man had evidently become aware of the approach of Minera's troops. He'd come to a halt, one hand raised high overhead in a cautionary signal. The flankers were moving discreetly forward, attention riveted to the front.

Bolan quickly seized the moment to make his move, coming up silently behind the right flank with weapons sheathed, stiletto in hand. He took the trailing flanker with a choke hold at the throat, pulling him expertly into the long blade of the stiletto. The guy died quietly in Bolan's embrace, aorta severed cleanly even as the larynx collapsed under the crushing choke hold, the departure unnoticed by his comrades. Bolan took his place and moved on with the others as the cautious advance continued.

He was a heartbeat away from tagging the next man when Minera lost his play on the other side. No discredit to the security chief—the terrain was uneven and the night alternately raven black—he stumbled or slid or did some clumsy thing to produce noise enough even for Bolan's distant awareness. The flankers on Bolan's side did not catch it but those three on the other side came around quickly with weapons at the ready.

This was, yeah, the kind of stuff flashbacks are made of.

The silent Beretta was in Bolan's big paw before there was time for the conscious mind to send the signal. It sneezed twice with hardly a gap between the two, dispatching twin 9mm projectiles across that no-man's-land to the left flank, instantly taking out the two Iranians on that side who were the farthest removed from Minera. The Security Chief under his own combat impetus was already furiously upon the third man with his bare hands.

It was at this point that Bolan lost track of Minera. He had problems enough of his own. The two remaining flankers on his side were now fully alert to the situation. They were scrambling, flinging themselves groundward in opposing directions while screaming warnings to the others. Meanwhile, the point man and those in the center had become occupied with Minera's three-man squad up front—and the night had come alive with the booming and chattering of combat weapons in open conflict.

Bolan himself was instinctively on the move, quitting his position as expertly triangulated fire

raked the ground behind him. It was not a retreat but a planned withdrawal. Minera had
been instructed to fall back to the pool area as
soon as hot contact was made. Whether or not
the guy was in any shape to do so was still a
question...and Bolan could not wait around
for the answer. The three-man security patrol
had at least a fighting chance now. Maybe they
would succeed in pinning these guys to the
ground here, and there was even the possibility
that they could drive them back or maybe even
wipe them out. Bolan was not betting on any of
that, however, and this particular commando
team could be but one of several others also on
the advance.

So he was not retreating, no. He was, in fact,
advancing to the next line of heat.

He had covered about half that distance
when the wheezing, disheveled security chief re-
joined.

"Jesus Christ!" Minera panted as he jogged
alongside.

"Make that a prayer," Bolan suggested.

"How many did we get?"

"Not nearly enough," the big man told him.
"Four...maybe five."

"So what do we do now?"

"Now," Bolan replied quietly, "we do or
die."

"I'll take do," Minera said.

"Or you could just bail out," said Bolan, giving the guy a quick, hard toss of the eyes.

"What the hell you think I am?" the security boss growled.

"I guess," Bolan muttered to himself, "I'm going to find that out damn quick."

And he probably would not like the answer. No, probably not any part of the answer.

The cabana was a solid brick structure, ten by ten, with a wooden ladder leading up to a sun deck on the roof.

Bolan started toward the ladder as he spoke over his shoulder. "Get back to the house," he instructed Minera. "There are four men on that squad unaccounted for."

Minera hesitated. "You're still not sure what happened to the general's brother, are you?"

Bolan was about to tell the guy that this was no time for conversing. But before he could speak, the sound of handguns, definitely more than one, carried from inside the main house.

Minera whipped around toward the sound. "Damn! Sounds like I'm too late!"

The gunfire from the house continued.

Other rounds were slapping into the far side of the cabana as the teams out front continued to advance, peppering the air before them.

"Forget trying to solve the murder," Bolan told the security man. "Get back to the house and give your boys some backup."

"What about you? Let's fall back together. There's six men closing in on you from out front!"

With one hand Bolan hefted himself up the ladder onto the sun deck, while he carried the M1 in the other.

"Suit yourself," he told Minera. "There's nothing you can do at this range with that .44. You can keep low and hide here, or you can fall back and help your men."

More rounds whistled into and around the small building. Some rounds made deadened *plop* noises as they hit the tarp covering the pool.

Bolan's analysis of Minera as a fighting man proved correct.

"I'm on my way," he called up to Bolan. He took off at a sprint around the darkened pool toward the big house.

The gunfire from the house had become more sporadic but was continuing, as if one faction had pulled back but was still giving resistance.

Bolan fell prone on the sun deck and through the Startron began scanning the driveway area for targets, to keep the commando teams busy while Minera made his run.

The firing between the guard patrol and the commandos on the right flank had died down to occasional rifle fire in the night.

The hail of incoming bullets at Bolan's position had intensified.

Bolan sighted in on the commandos to the right flank, who were engaging Minera's dog patrol. He flicked the M1's shot—this time for the grenade launcher.

He yanked one of the SAS-style flash grenades from the belt across his chest and fed it into the launcher with practiced precision.

The hellfire here tonight had only just begun.

12

From Mack Bolan's journal:

Moral shades of gray can be very troubling. I much prefer the simple black and white situation of the mafia wars, when there was never any question as to who the enemy was.

This guy Nazarour is as big a shark as any I've ever encountered. It really bruises the soul to have to keep a man like this alive. In basic black and white, the guy should die. But I no longer deal just in basics. For the moment—for a very limited moment, I hope—the complications of world politics have lent a synthetic virtue to his presence here on American soil. So... for now... the man must live, and I must do everything in my power to ensure that he does. But, yeah, it bruises the soul just a bit.

My feelings for the man have nothing to do with where he comes from, or whom he served while he was there. The same goes for my feelings regarding the job at hand. The whole truth of the matter is that there is no moral issue in Iran, at this moment. I hope that one day soon

there will be. As of now, though, what is happening there is a contest between savages...
with neither side morally superior to the other.
Were it not for the fact that it is always the innocents who suffer most in any such situation, I
would say: let the world draw a curtain around
Iran and let the savages have at one another
until there are none left—or until the good
people finally rise up and smash the savages one
and all. But it does not appear that anything like
that will be happening in the foreseeable future,
so we who are on the sidelines will just have to
do what we can to keep the game as clean as
possible in whatever limited way that we may.
This is the thinking that led me to accept the
present mission. I do not want Iranian hit
squads roaming this country looking for targets.
I do not want their war on our territory. So I
am here, and I intend to do what I can to discourage any future operations of this nature. It
does not mean that I approve of Nazarour or
anything that he may stand for. It simply means
that I cannot turn my back on what is happening here.

At the same time, I have to keep the mind
alert and the options open. Everything is not as
it appears to be. . . .

There is the question of the general's wife:
precisely what is her situation and precisely
what could or should I do about her?

And then, of course, there is Minera. Shades of gray, indeed. This particular picture appears to be focusing more along the classic lines of black and white. My mental radar picks up strong mafia blips every time I look at the guy. So what is he to Nazarour? And what is Nazarour to him?

Well...the answers will come. And I have the feeling that when they do, the shades of gray will all resolve into strong patterns of opposing colors, and black and white. Then all the options will have narrowed to one.

13

"Striker, this is Stony Man on channel bravo. Do you read?"

For the past seven minutes Hal Brognola had been droning on with that single phrase into the transceiver of the radio set.

April Rose stood behind Hal, trying to ward off the chills that she knew had nothing to do with the temperature in Stony Man Farm's command room.

Hal grunted a curse and tossed the transceiver onto the counter with an angry clatter.

"Damn. We're not getting through at all. He's either deactivated his set or jammed the frequency on the other end."

There was another possibility, of course. But April knew that she didn't have to remind Hal of that other alternative. She tried not to think about it herself.

"The attack may be coming down right now and he's too busy to respond," she said with a confidence that sounded forced even to her own ears. "He'll get back to us."

Hal nodded acknowledgment without turning from the radio. "I just wish we could get through to him."

"You think it's that important, the information about those men he killed at the canal earlier tonight?"

"The fact that they were all Americans—the fact that according to our man in Org Crime they are a direct franchise of what's left of the local Family since Striker's last swing through here—yeah, I think it's plenty important that he know.

"They're Mafia torpedoes. Now where the hell would they fit in? This thing gets screwier and screwier."

April stepped forward and touched featherlight fingertips to the boss's shoulder.

"Hal...."

The fed chuckled mildly. He reached across with his left hand and patted those fingertips.

"I know, April. Cool down and easy does it. But we've got to keep trying."

Then, with his right hand, he brought the transceiver back to his mouth and began repeating over and over again, "Striker, this is Stony Man on channel bravo. Do you read?"

April pulled back and returned to her own chair. She couldn't shake the feeling somewhere deep inside that all hell was breaking loose at this moment, ninety miles north in Potomac.

The feeling was tearing her guts to shreds.

At that moment, the man she cared about was probably fighting for his life.

The big, beautiful man named Mack Bolan who had come into her world and touched her soul and changed that world forever.

A man who had taught her the true meaning of the words *sacrifice* and *concern*.

Yes, it was happening in Potomac at this minute.

She could *feel* it.

But all she could do was sit and wait. And hope. And try not to think about bad things.

Bolan was playing the enemy's game, doing his best to take *them* by surprise. Keep them guessing.

A quick scan up-range had shown that two of Minera's guard patrol had been hit. One was wounded but returning sporadic fire; the other appeared dead. One looked okay in the scope's greenish tint.

The commandos hadn't sustained any losses yet. The remaining terrorists to Bolan's right were returning the guard patrol's fire.

Team Number Two continued advancing along the left side of the driveway, moving steadily from approximately five hundred yards. These three were still sending occasional rounds toward the pool area and the front of the house, but they hadn't spotted Bolan on his perch atop the cabana.

The big warrior changed all that.

He triggered the M1 and sent a flash grenade zinging into the right flank of the team. The grenade went off with a blinding flare. When Bolan looked up from shielding his eyes to the flash, the first thing he saw was the three men standing out from behind their cover and clawing at scorched eyes, oblivious to everything but their pain.

Bolan readjusted the M1's selector mode and squeezed off a round. That dropped the first of the stunned commandos.

One of the guards got off a shot at that point, and another Iranian grunted and pitched flat onto his face, lying motionless.

Number Three finally got some sense and flattened out of sight.

The guard patrol would have to handle that one, Bolan decided. He had other priorities. Such as the squad advancing along the left side of the driveway.

He saw through the scope from about four hundred yards that two of them were toting the RPG-7. They were in the process of pulling away from him, falling farther away to the left. Their plan seemed to be to cut around the far end of the pool, away from Bolan, and come around in front of the main house via the cobblestone walk.

That *was* the plan.

Except that Bolan had exposed his position by firing the flash grenade.

In one smooth movement that resembled an acrobatic exercise, the big warrior and the M1 and Uzi were off the cabana roof without benefit of the wooden steps.

Bolan landed gracefully and sped off in the direction of the house, hugging the opposite side of the pool from the commando team, following the path that Minera had taken a few minutes earlier.

He jogged along low and fast and had covered close to ten yards when the RPG-7 belched smoke and noise in the distance.

One second later the cabana on which Bolan had been perched only seconds before exploded in another nightmare of sound and spewing brick and glass.

Bolan continued along the cobblestone walk, skirting the edge of the pool, passing the body of Dr. Nazarour with barely a sideward glance. The body appeared as he had last seen it.

Gunfire continued to echo from inside the house.

The commandos out front would now be continuing on toward the house from their own side of the pool. Bolan's actions and decisions in the next few seconds could well determine the outcome of this fight.

He reached the cabana situated at the end of the pool closest to the house. He had won the race with the terrorists who were advancing from the other side of the swimming pool.

The cabana stood three hundred feet from the house. The sun deck would afford a view of the hit squad's approach, as well as of the side windows of the main house, which was probably their destination.

Bolan knew there were only heartbeats left now until that squad would be moving into view in the moonlight. They must have written him off as dead from the rocket attack on the other cabana.

Strapping the M1 over the shoulder opposite the Uzi, Bolan moved to the area of ground between the cabana and the house, over which the squad would have to approach if Bolan's reading of their strategy was correct.

He was a blurred shadow in the darkness. When he reached a spot midway between house and cabana, he paused and reached into the pouch that had been riding at his left hip. He carefully withdrew the curved metallic body of a portable claymore antipersonnel mine. He positioned the mine on the ground so as to cover the approach of the expected team, pointing it away from the cabana. The object was indistinguishable in the nighttime shadows.

The snap of a twig ten yards off told Bolan

how little time he had left. He had gained some seconds by his jog around the pool. But they were still coming. Almost on top of him.

Call it twenty seconds on the outside.

All at once he was aware that the gunfire from inside the house had ceased.

He continued preparing the surprise, unrolling a long strip of pressure-sensitive detonation tape and running it across the width of ground where he expected Yazid's men to pass. Then, with all due care and pressing speed, he connected the wires of the trigger tape to the mine. With seven seconds to spare, he reeled around and got the hell out of there, back to the cabana, taking the wooden steps on the run and sprawling out flat across the roof of the sun deck. He swung the M1 back and around, sighting through the Startron to pinpoint the enemy.

He made out the three-man team clearly enough. They were practically on top of the detonation tape, but not quite. He probably could have taken them out from his perch, but with three-to-one odds and all of them pros, Bolan had chosen to take all three at once, and that was still seconds away from happening.

He swung the rifle up-range until the Startron sighted in on the cobblestone pathway alongside the pool. It picked up one commando moving in along that route. He must have recovered from the flash grenade that Bolan had sent his way.

He was no doubt headed toward the house to join his teammates.

Bolan triggered off a round at the lone man. Again it was one round, one kill. The Startron magnified in pale green the awful impact of missile on flesh. Bone structure turned to fading mist as the guy was yanked off his feet as if he had been shoved backward over a low wire.

The M1 packed its usual mighty recoil, but the explosive report was drowned out as the HE below on Bolan's left was triggered by one of the commandos tripping the detonation tape.

In a night full of hell's fire, the claymore had a power all its own. That other cabana seemed to shake beneath Bolan. But the chief benefit of the claymore is that its blast can be aimed in a specific direction.

Bolan rose up to one knee without fear of being hit by debris. He set aside the M1 and swung up the Uzi for a fast cleanup.

The mighty blast of the antipersonnel mine was rolling across the Maryland hills, echoing off into the night.

It was a bloody mess down there below the cabana. The Iranians had come to this land to deliver horror. And that's what they had received.

The top half of a torso, most of its head gone, had pitched against the base of a tree.

A lone shoe, the foot inside it taken off at

mid-ankle, smoldered on the ground all by it-self.

Two relatively intact bodies were thrashing around wildly on their backs like crushed insects.

Screams of pain and the smell of burned flesh filled the air.

Bolan sprayed the two bodies with a quick burst from the Uzi.

The screaming stopped.

Death was their business, huh?

Now they could sample the goods.

The final echoes of battle, that last chatter from the Uzi, receded into the distance. And with that—as abruptly as that—the battle seemed to be over. Peace again reigned over Potomac.

Sure it did. . . .

Bolan climbed down from his cabana. He crossed over and slung the M1 in through the window of his parked Vette. The Uzi was what was called for now. The ideal weapon for quick spurts in tight areas. For indoor fighting.

There was still, after all, no way of telling why the gunfire had ceased inside the main house.

Bolan moved to the house and entered silently through a ground-floor window.

All he found inside were dead men.

The walls of the front hallway and the study

where Bolan had left General Nazarour were riddled with holes and splashed with blood.

The dead men included one commando and the two security guards that Bolan had left behind to guard the general.

Bolan hurriedly, methodically, searched the house from top to bottom.

There was no sign of the general. Or of Rafsanjani. Or of Carol Nazarour. Or of Minera.

They were gone.

14

The three of them sat around a table in the kitchen, one of the few rooms on the ground floor of the house that had not been scathed in the battle. The greenhouse had gone entirely.

Hal Brognola's expression was a mixture of profound relief at seeing Bolan alive and concern regarding the mission.

"You called it right on how they busted in," he reported. Brognola had just come in from supervising the cleanup detail outside. "They knocked out the guards in Gatehouse Two out there with nerve gas. Someone who had access to the gatehouse planted the canisters beforehand. Kilgore from the lab took a look at 'em and said they were probably triggered tonight by a radio signal from somewhere in the immediate vicinity.

"I'd say that narrows it down to somebody who was here among you tonight. A classic inside job."

April Rose frowned. "But who? Everyone here this evening was dependent on the general for his security or his job. It doesn't make sense."

As soon as they arrived, Bolan had briefed Brognola and April on the details of what had gone down here tonight. At the moment Bolan was sipping coffee that April had prepared for the three of them. It was helping to revive him, which was something he sorely needed at that moment. Now that the pumping adrenalin of the fight had subsided, the weariness was beginning to crawl back over him again. It had been a long time since Mack Bolan's last full eight hours of sleep. But he couldn't slow down. Not yet.

The fighting here in Potomac was over.

But the mission was not.

The big warrior had made a promise to Carol Nazarour. He had promised her that he would see her clear of this nest of vipers. Now she had disappeared, sure. She had gone somewhere with her dear, deadly husband and Minera and Rafsanjani. With them, yeah—but against her will. Bolan could read the situation no other way. If she was all right, Carol Nazarour would have been sitting there in the kitchen with them right now. Beretta or no, she had been overpowered and forced to accompany the others.

When Bolan thought about that, the adrenalin started pumping again, and he knew he had it in him to keep going until this thing was wrapped up.

After verifying that General Nazarour and his group had indeed disappeared, Bolan's first step had been to activate his hip radio and call in the Stony Man team. In minutes waiting choppers had ferried the cigar-chewing top cop and April to the Potomac mansion. Accompanying them had been the team of federal marshals under Hal's command, who were presently outside tagging bodies and canvassing the property. It was early dawn.

"What was the body count?" Bolan asked quietly.

"Twenty-one," Hal replied. "The guards were wiped out, and the hit team left their dead behind. Eleven of 'em."

"Have you tagged any of them as the leader?"

"Unfortunately, no. Looks like you pretty well nullified the guy's operation, but the head man, Yazid, made it clean. So did Amir Pouyan, his second-in-command."

"They must have been leading the team that swung around into the house while I was busy with the squads out front," Bolan said. "That means that both General Nazarour and this Yazid are on the loose out there somewhere today."

"I've got men covering the airstrip in Rockville where Nazarour was supposed to catch his plane this morning," said Brognola. "Though I doubt if he'll show. He'll probably figure that if

Yazid found him here, then he's probably hip to the whole layout, plane and all.''

"And he probably is," Bolan added. "How did Yazid's men breach the security at the gate out front?''

Hal spoke as he poured them each another cup of coffee. "Same M.O. as the inside gatehouse. Cyanide, except with gas guns. It was easy. They took the guard when he came up to the car to check their ID! Then they opened up on the other guards. That was the firing you say Minera heard. The guards in Gatehouse Two were already knocked out from the planted canisters, so Yazid's people just walked in. And we got what we wanted—a shot at a hit team. The men at Number One didn't stand a chance.''

Bolan stared down into his coffee for a moment, as if it might give him the right words to express what he was thinking.

"The guys who were guarding this place fought the good fight," he said finally. "The ones inside who were given half a chance fought with everything they had until their numbers ran out. Whatever the backgrounds on those people, Hal, they fought and died like men.''

"But I still don't understand the connection between the general and a security crew that happens to be a franchise of the Maryland Mafia,'' April broke in. "Was it a coincidence?''

"Nothing's coincidental in Washington, April," Bolan reminded her. "The connection is money. This house was furnished for the general's use by some friends he had made in high places when the Shah was in power. Friends who obviously still want to keep the general alive and comfortable. And these friends have friends. That's who they turned to when they wanted to recruit security for the general. A lot of people in this town aren't too particular about who their friends are."

"And it was some of Minera's own men who were trying to kidnap Mrs. Nazarour when you showed up last night?"

Bolan nodded. The events under discussion—that sudden firefight at the Chesapeake & Ohio Canal, in which six other men had died—had gone down only scant hours before. Yet in some ways it seemed to Bolan as if a great passage of time had transpired. So much had happened. So much death.

"Yeah, they were Minera's boys," he replied. "The general is in the habit of having punishments administered to his wife. The lady was having an affair with one of the guards, and of course Minera found out about it and told the general. The general arranged to have the man killed tonight in front of his wife's eyes, then have the wife kidnapped and. . . punished before they left the country tomorrow morning. Or maybe he'd grown tired of her. Maybe he didn't care what happened to her.

"He was willing to let her go easily enough in a conversation we had just prior to attack."

"It's too bad it was your job to defend the general," said April with quiet intensity. "It sounds as if the creep deserved everything that was coming to him."

Bolan was amused at the increasing vehemence of this fine woman, who had joined the Stony Man team only months ago.

"I still don't give much of a damn about the general," he told her. "His past will catch up with him soon enough, one way or another. But Mrs. Nazarour reached out to me. I promised her that I'd help. I *will* help her, any way I can.

"I just hope something comes in that we can follow up, and fast. If Karim Yazid is running leads down faster than we are, or if he's luckier than we've been and he's located the general and his party, then he's going to give everything he's got to carrying out his original mission to hit Nazarour. In a situation like that, the general's wife will probably be dead before we can get to her."

April leaned forward and touched Bolan's hand across the table. She spoke in that soft voice which could convey so much strength.

"You're doing the right thing," she assured him. "And you've been pushing so hard for so long. There's nothing you can do right now but wait for that phone on the wall to ring. Hal's men are doing everything they can. You should use this time to rest. You'll need your strength later."

She was right, of course, Bolan reflected. April Rose, along with Hal, was one of the few people whose judgment Bolan trusted implicitly. He made the decisions, sure. But he always listened to what April said.

Brognola struck a match and relit his ever present stogie. "Please don't you two start making moon eyes at each other," he begged in mock desperation, through a cloud of cigar smoke. "How about trying to figure out who killed the general's brother out there by the pool? There's a healthy pastime. Any ideas on that?"

Before Bolan could respond, April added to the question. "And how many bad guys are we dealing with here? Is the person who killed Dr. Nazarour the same person who planted the cyanide canisters in the gatehouse out front?"

"Yeah, they were the same person," said Bolan. "My guess is that Dr. Nazarour came across the guilty party out there by the swimming pool just as the person was triggering the radio signal to release the cyanide in the gatehouse. I don't know what the general's brother was doing out there. I had it figured that he'd be in his room, junked out on something. But somehow he ended up out there just before the fighting commenced, and somehow he got himself killed."

Brognola snorted. A sour sound. "Whatever happened to the old-time simple missions?" he asked rhetorically. "This damn thing has more angles than a—"

He was interrupted by the ringing of the kitchen wall phone. Bolan stood and grabbed it.

"Hello?"

"Colonel Phoenix? Thank God it's you. This is Carol Nazarour. I—I need you...." The voice came in a panicky, hushed whisper. She must have been praying that it was Bolan who would answer the phone in her beleaguered home.

"Where are you?" he asked.

"At a restaurant in Bannockburn Heights. Do you know where that is?"

Bolan knew. "Where are they taking you?"

"To a small airstrip in Bethesda."

"Bethesda? That's all residential or government property."

"There's supposed to be a very short airfield near the naval hospital," she told him. "They use it for STOLs—that's what Minera called them—whatever they are."

"Short Takeoff and Landing," said Bolan. "There's a field on Goldsboro that the hospital uses. Is there any way you can break away now?''

''No. I'm in the ladies' room. Rafsanjani is waiting for me outside the door. He doesn't know there's a phone in here. I was trying to escape on my own. I knew the tunnel was useless because Eshan would probably have someone guarding it. I was holding your gun and cutting off from the ground when Rafsanjani took me by surprise from behind. I never heard him. He moved like a cat! He took the gun and—*oh, my God! No!...*''

Bolan heard a flurry of motion on the line. The distinct sound of flesh being brutally slapped.

The line went dead.

Hal and April were both watching Bolan keenly as he hung up the phone and swung around.

''It was her, wasn't it?'' said April.

Bolan nodded. ''There's an airstrip in Bethesda. The general's on his way there to meet his flight. That's where the action is.''

Brognola rose and started with Bolan toward the door. ''Let me get some of the boys together and we'll—''

Bolan stopped him with a slight touch on the arm. ''No, Hal. I've got to do this alone.''

''Alone?'' Brognola obviously had not expected this from Bolan, but he fielded it smoothly. "No way, buddy. Yazid and what's left of his Iranian attack force could show up at that airstrip. You've done more than your share already, Striker. You've got to let me back you up on this one."

But Bolan was adamant.

"Hal, that lady's life is my chief priority at this point," he told the fed. "Don't worry, I'm not forgetting Yazid and his bunch. Maybe they're onto the general, maybe they're not. But either way, I am going to get Mrs. Nazarour safely out of that situation she's in.

"If Yazid and his sidekick Pouyan are there and I show up with a cadre of federal marshals and the shooting starts—well, the idea is to get the woman *safely* away from there, not get her killed in action."

April spoke from where she sat at the table. "He's right, Hal. We have to let him do it his way."

Brognola snorted with mock gruffness. "Don't we always. Okay, Striker. We'll fall in as backup a mile to your rear. I trust that will be giving you enough room to swing?"

"That'll give me plenty of room," said Bolan grimly. "Thanks for understanding, Hal. Okay, let's roll."

He lifted a clenched fist as a final silent "Stay hard" to these fellow warriors on the team.

Then he was off and moving into the night again.

For one more confrontation possibly with two separate enemies.

He was pushing himself to the max and he knew it.

But there was no way he could shrug off his responsibility to Carol Nazarour.

No way at all.

Bolan knew in his gut that the coming confrontation would be fast, bloody, and decisive. And it was less than thirty minutes away.

No more sitting by the phone.

The game was again in play.

15

Karim Yazid was slowly coming out of his state of shock. The slaughter of his men on the grounds of the estate in Potomac had left him stunned and responding purely at an instinctual level.

The Iranian hit-squad leader vaguely remembered fleeing that scene with Amir. There had been staunch resistance inside the house from the guards protecting the general. The guards had fallen, along with one of Karim and Amir's squad. Then Minera, whom Yazid had once met through Rafsanjani, had arrived in the house. The security chief had been a mighty fighter, and somehow he had spirited the general and his party away.

But the ferocity of Minera had been nothing compared to the level of resistance encountered by the three squads of Karim's men who had attacked the front of the house.

The scene of dismembered bodies where the claymore had been detonated had sickened both Karim and Amir. From that point on, Karim's memory became hazy. He remembered running silently with Amir toward the front gate. He remembered, as if it were a dream, passing the bodies of his men, which lay stretched across the property of that estate.

These images somehow became interspersed in his mind with images of that climactic day of the '79 revolution, when these same fourteen men of his squad had stormed the Lavizan barracks in northeastern Tehran. It had been their finest moment, as these tough commandos had outmaneuvered and slain scores of the Shah's crack *Javidan* guards in one bloody sweep through their fortress compound. Now, on an estate in Maryland, these men had gone to Allah. They had died with weapons in their hands. Martyrs to the cause of Islam.

And Karim Yazid was left without a team. At first he could not believe what he had heard from the lone survivor of the front assault squads—a badly wounded man whom Karim and Amir had carried between them on the final leg of their trek out through the front gates of the estate, to where one of their vans had been parked nearby.

The man had mumbled that only one man had delivered all of this devastation to Yazid's crack team.

One man!

Karim remembered pulling away in the van to

the shrieking of sirens that had been approaching from all directions in response to the sounds of open warfare.

Slowly, the images of then evolved to the present.

Karim blinked and stared at the restaurant out through the front window of the van.

He knew now where he was. He knew what he had to do.

Luck had finally shone on Karim as he, Amir, and the wounded man had fled in the van. Karim had hardly driven forty feet when he spotted a car pulling away from a cluster of shrubbery below and alongside the road, where the car had been hidden.

Karim fell back and followed the car, a sleek new Mercedes.

He could not shake the certainty that he was following General Nazarour and company.

The cries of the wounded commando had filled the van. Amir administered a shot of pain killer, and the cries had subsided to low, unintelligible murmurs.

Karim had followed the car into Bannockburn Heights, and at a twenty-four-hour restaurant on River Road, Karim's suspicions had been confirmed.

He watched as Rafsanjani, that hellion Minera, the general himself, and Mrs. Nazarour had gone into the restaurant. From a point halfway up the block, Karim had continued observing them with binoculars through the plate-glass window of the restaurant.

The conversation between the four had been fervent and secretive. Minera had left the party for several minutes. He returned to make a report. Karim was sure that they were lining up another flight out of the country. A few minutes later, a scene had transpired during which it appeared that Mrs. Nazarour was being discreetly but severely chastised for something she had done.

The important thing to Karim, sitting there behind the wheel of the van, was that he was still on the general. There was still hope for the mission.

He had to isolate the general's party. There were two rounds remaining for the rocket launcher. But he had to choose his spot carefully for the ambush if he wished to make a successful withdrawal. Karim did not underestimate the efficiency of the local police agencies in the face of an event such as the one that had occurred that night in Potomac. All neighboring precincts would be on alert.

Karim decided that the best time to assassinate his target would be as the general was actually boarding the plane that was to fly him out of the country. There was a risk involved, certainly. The risk that something would go wrong, without a second chance. But the general's group seemed to be unaccompanied by additional security. That man Minera was a worthy fighter, true. But he would be one man against a rocket launcher. And in an open area such as an airfield, the chances of a clean withdrawal were practically guaranteed. The risk would be minimal, when compared with trying to make the attack on a city street.

It was only a matter of time. A matter of following the general from the restaurant to whatever airstrip Nazarour had engaged for his rescheduled departure.

Yazid became aware that the murmurings of the wounded man in the back of the van had ceased. Yazid turned from the steering wheel as Amir moved forward and sank into the passenger seat alongside him.

"He's dead," Amir reported quietly. "It's down to the two of us now, Karim."

Karim looked back in the direction of the restaurant. The general's group was in the process of leaving. The Iranians could see Abbas Rafsanjani through the window, paying the tab at the cash register. Soon the party would be back in the Mercedes.

Then to the airfield.

And that was where they would die.

As he watched the group move hastily from the restaurant to the car, Amir hissed, "We should kill them now for what they have done to our brothers!''

''Be patient, my friend,'' Karim replied. ''They will die. But not here. I have considered the matter. We could not get away. You must trust me.''

''I do trust you, Karim,'' the lieutenant said, and he lapsed into silence.

Karim Yazid also fell into thought as the general's car, driven by Minera, exited the restaurant parking lot, turned south onto River Road, and continued toward Bethesda.

Karim fell in at ten car lengths behind the Mercedes, and continued tailing the general's group through the quiet early-morning streets of Washington suburbia.

The cold gray traces of dawn were lighting the eastern horizon. There were a few more vehicles on the streets, but that was just as well. More traffic meant better camouflage.

As he drove, Karim Yazid's mind shifted to the factor that he and Amir had avoided discussing.

Who was that individual who had wrought such havoc among the three frontal-assault teams? It must have been the man whom Amir had seen returning with Mrs. Nazarour earlier that night. But *who* was he? And would he appear at the final confrontation at the airstrip?

For reasons of his own, General Nazarour appeared intent on eluding this mysterious figure. Very well. That would be the error that would seal the general's fate.

And if this mysterious fighting man did appear?

Yazid thought of the dead comrades he had left behind in Potomac. A part of him fervently hoped that this man *would* make another appearance.

There was a blood debt to be settled.

But either way, the general would die.

To the south, within the residential section of Bethesda through which Karim had been tracking the Mercedes, the open expanse of an airfield loomed into view.

It would happen soon.

Karim Yazid was prepared to meet his fate and to deliver the general's fate.

This time he and Amir would not fail.

Nazarour, his wife, Rafsanjani, Minera—they would all die.

But even as he felt the prekill iciness begin to creep over him, Karim Yazid could not free himself of two lingering questions. Who was the warrior in black? And where was he now?

16

River Road was just beginning to clog with commuter traffic as Bolan caught the Goldsboro Road turn and continued on the hilly roller-coasterlike stretch with the Corvette's gas pedal floored, racing through suburban residential neighborhoods on a direct course toward the Bethesda Naval Hospital district.

It was 6:18 A.M.

The sun had risen minutes earlier like an ornamental silver disc in the eastern sky. The warmth of the newborn sunlight hadn't penetrated his car yet. And even with the heater on, Bolan felt chilled to the bone. The world outside looked grim and bleak.

Bolan held the Corvette at fifty miles per hour, playing morning traffic, moving smoothly in and out of lanes, unobtrusively gaining every second he could.

This had become a personal matter for the big man with the icy eyes—this race against time to intercept General Nazarour's group before they could rendezvous with the plane that would whisk them out of the country.

Bolan had no idea what would happen at this confrontation. But he would damn sure be finding out, within short minutes.

The two leaders of the Iranian hit squad that had been this mission's original top priority were still on the loose, and Bolan felt that there was a good chance he would encounter them ahead also. If Yazid and Pouyan were not about to make an appearance, then they could be anywhere in the D.C. area. But tracking them down was no longer a one-man job. Hal's forces were working on that end.

Helping Carol Nazarour was another matter entirely.

It was, yes, a personal matter.

Due both to the fact that Bolan had expressly promised his assistance to the lady, and to the fact that he could not help but see Carol Nazarour as a living symbol, if there ever was one, of just what this whole "new war" was about.

Mack Bolan did not see himself as a do-gooder, crusader, or zealot of any sort. He was a man who simply could not coexist peaceably with flagrant human savagery. Bolan's high-school yearbook showed a picture of an intense young man, captioned: "He can because he must." Hindsight revealed a basic misunderstanding in the mind of the caption writer. The caption should have read: "He must because he can." Mack Bolan's entire existence was based on commitment. It was his reason for being. Commitment to ideals, to *doing* something in service to those ideals, to making some contribution to the human estate, to the evolutionary process, to living to his full potential—these were what gave his life meaning.

His commitment was based on a simple philosophical stand.

The savages—Yazid and all of these other merchants of terror everywhere—had to be fought back. The baseness and inherent self-destructiveness of aggression could not be endured by a civilization that had dreamed of touching the stars and had made those dreams come true, and had the potential for reaching so much more.

Yet, ironically, only force could subdue savagery. Force, used with discretion and conviction.

In Bolan's sharp perception of the situation, his own expertise and combat capabilities not only qualified him for the task but made mandatory his commitment as a champion of the human cause.

There were times, sure, when the spirit lagged. When he longed for the freedom of irresponsibility. When he would have liked nothing better than to just kick back and let go and let the world find its own level without his input. But Mack Bolan understood that the world was not made *for* people but *by* people. He was responsible for the world in which he found himself. And there was no rest for such a man.

A heavy concept, sure.

But simple also. The new war was a war between evolution and devolution.

17

Bolan swung the Corvette's padded steering wheel, cutting off Goldsboro Road onto the blacktopped approach to the landing field. The naval hospital towered in the distance.

It was 6:30 A.M.

The open expanse of ground sitting in this residential area made Bolan think of a playing field of some sort. The autumn grass separating the short runways was burnished to a coppery gold by the morning sunlight.

There was no gate barring entrance. The Vette passed the chain-link fence that ran the perimeter of the field.

Bolan lifted his foot gently from the gas pedal. His gaze took a quick survey of the acreage—four hundred yards by three-quarters of a mile—that engulfed him.

He spotted the STOL and General Nazarour's group immediately.

One hundred and fifty yards to the east.

The craft, a Sky Terrier, all wings and stubby fuselage, quivered on the tarmac like an arrow drawn tight against its bow, ready to be fired. From the look of the pilot and crew, dimly visible from where Bolan was, the craft had been hired or otherwise appropriated by a team of Arabs, presumably in league with Nazarour.

The general's Mercedes had entered the field via an entrance opposite the Goldsboro Road access that Bolan had used. The Mercedes was midway between that opposite entrance and the waiting plane. The driver was in a hurry.

Bolan's mind rapidly computed his chances of intercepting the Mercedes before it reached the STOL. Once the Mercedes made the plane, there would be no screwing around. It would be out of the car and onto the plane and gone.

Yeah.

Gone.

Just like Bolan's promise to Carol Nazarour that he would help her.

But even as Bolan's foot coaxed more fuel into the car's engine, accelerating for a dead run across the field to intercept the Mercedes, movement from the periphery of his vision brought Bolan's attention to some forty yards behind the Mercedes.

A blue panel van had come barreling along the tarmac through that opposite entrance, in hot pursuit of the Mercedes.

Karim Yazid. Amir Pouyan. The Iranians.

Bolan was faced with a decision of the damned.

Now it figured why the Mercedes was in such a hammer-down hurry.

The occupants of the Mercedes knew they were being pursued.

The Iranian assassins were closing in for the kill.

The van didn't speed more than a few yards onto the field. Then it swerved into a sideways skid and shimmied to a halt.

Bolan saw two men leap out from opposite sides of the van. The two were still togged in their nighttime commando gear, as was Bolan. He couldn't make out every detail from this distance, but he could see that the two men were lugging equipment behind them, which they hurriedly began setting up alongside the van, facing the Mercedes and the plane. Some hundred and thirty yards separated them from their target. But the two didn't seem concerned about that.

Of course.

They had the RPG-7 rocket launcher that had wrought such destruction last night in the hellground in Potomac.

Back for an encore.

The driver of the Mercedes apparently hadn't seen Bolan yet. He had eyes only for what was happening in his rearview mirror back by the van. The Mercedes picked up speed, moving even more rapidly toward the waiting STOL.

Bolan floored the gas and sent the sleek sports car hurtling toward Yazid and Pouyan.

The final stretch of pavement between the Mercedes and the awaiting STOL curved and ran parallel to the van parked across the field.

The general's car presented a perfect target as it sped past the blank white faces of a row of hangars.

Bolan's Corvette was reaching maximum speed. The machine's powerful engine screamed in his ears as it thrust him across the golden turf toward the van.

The two men had completed setting up the RPG-7. They were sighting and preparing to fire.

For the first time they heard the approaching sports car and in unison swung startled glances over their shoulders.

Bolan could feel the steering wheel furrowing his palms, just as the tires were digging furrows into the grassy ground beneath him.

It would be tight, yeah.

Yazid and Pouyan exchanged frantic words.

The Corvette came on relentlessly.

Bolan spared a sideways glance.

The Mercedes also was eating up time and space. Bolan calculated its present distance from the STOL at about thirty yards and closing fast.

Real tight.

Seconds flew by like the last grains of sand dropping through an hourglass—impersonal, oblivious to human drama or even life itself.

As Bolan's vehicle swallowed up the distance between him and the van, the big soldier reached across and grabbed the Uzi from where it had been riding on the seat beside him.

He was practically on top of the men by the van now.

They, too, had readjusted their priorities. The general and company seemed temporarily forgotten. The two Iranians in commando black hurriedly began shifting the RPG-7 around in an arc to line up on the approaching car.

When he was about seventy feet from the van, and while the two were still hassling with their gear, Bolan wrenched the Corvette off course yet again.

The car swerved in a wide half-circle, bringing Bolan abreast of the two men and still sailing.

With his right hand only, he continued steering while with his left he swung the Uzi up until its stubby snout was pointing out the window at the two men like an accusing finger.

The Iranian on the left moved faster than his buddy. He took a dive away from the rocket launcher and fell loosely into a roll that continued under the van and out of sight. Bolan had guessed from watching the two that this was

Yazid. He had been giving the orders. And he moved with the grace of a desert snake.

Out in the open, Amir Pouyan dropped into a crouch, grabbing for a side arm.

As Bolan sped past, the blurred impression of the Iranian's eyes and mouth flying open wide with the awful realization of approaching death registered for one instant.

Then the Uzi was chattering madly in Bolan's ears, and the hail of 9mm slugs was doing its work, rendering Pouyan's facial expression into exploding matter.

Amir Pouyan executed a wild jig of death as the Uzi ended his career as an Islamic assassin. Some of the bullets riddled the van behind him, splashing the side of the vehicle with a running mosaic of blood.

The Corvette sped by, missing the nose of the van by fractions of an inch. Bolan got a view of the other side of the van for the first time.

Karim Yazid had not remained under the van.

The last remaining terrorist of the commando team had moved around, retrieving the RPG-7 from the fallen Amir. He was now up on one knee in the classic bazooka firing stance, with the RPG-7 propped over his left shoulder.

Waiting for Bolan.

Bolan spotted Yazid at the exact moment that his car roared into the rocket launcher's range.

Bolan dropped the Uzi. He dropped the steer-

ing wheel. He dropped everything. He bent low
and, with the car still roaring, propelled himself
across the Corvette's front bucket seats, stiff-
arming the passenger door open and rolling
from the speeding vehicle at precisely the same
moment that he heard the booming of the
RPG-7.

Bolan hit the ground hard but rolling, keeping his perfectly conditioned body loose and
relaxed, carrying through with a roll that ended
with him upright on his feet and running at full
tilt, the mighty .44 AutoMag under his arm
seeming to leap into his right fist of its own voli-
tion.

But even as Bolan was rolling, then running,
the ground shook beneath him. The rocket
launcher's report was echoed and swallowed up
by the second, louder, explosion of the moving
Vette being blown into a wild ball of orange-red
fire and noise and fragmenting automobile.

Bolan felt chunks of debris flying by him, but
he didn't pay attention to that.

He was looking for Yazid.

There was no sign of the guy.

The commando leader had not waited around
to confirm the hit. The Iranian had been sure of
himself, and with damn good reason.

A worthy adversary, yeah. A deadly foe.

The engine of the van roared to life. Yazid
was apparently aborting the mission, forgetting

about the general and everything else except staying alive and getting the hell out of there. He was not the martyr type, apparently. The guy knew impossible resistance when he saw it, and all he wanted now was out.

The van lurched into gear and started pulling away, doing a U-turn that would take it back out the same way it had entered the airfield.

Bolan squeezed off a round intended for the van's left rear tire, but the vehicle jolted across a rut in the turf at that precise moment, and the slug only kicked up a clump of dirt inches to the left.

The Executioner was sighting for another shot when assistance arrived from a decidedly unexpected quarter.

The Mercedes carrying General Nazarour and his group came barreling in full speed from left field, literally. The driver pulled the car around in a sharp turn so that the Mercedes effectively blocked the van's intended route of retreat.

Yazid tried to avoid the collision by swerving to the left.

Bolan found himself tensing a split second before the inevitable crash filled the air with the sound of impacting metal on metal, mingled with shattering glass and human sounds.

The van hobbled away from the collision, slowing to a halt, while the Mercedes didn't seem to have sustained much more damage than a slightly dented front right fender.

The car had slewed away from the impact and also come to a stop.

Bolan moved fast toward the driver's side of the van. There was no movement from inside the cab. No silhouette of Karim Yazid's figure behind the wheel.

That was because Yazid had attempted Bolan's own maneuver, dropping out through the passenger side of the cab, which was facing away from Bolan.

The Iranian hit leader suddenly appeared from behind the van's tail. He held his Ingram. The deadly weapon was spraying the area where Bolan should have been.

Except that opponents don't fool Bolan with Bolan's own tactics.

At the first blur of movement from behind the van, before Karim Yazid had even been a discernible figure, Mack Bolan had dropped forward onto his belly in a prone firing position, his right fist supported by his left, both elbows propped up, and an iced blue eye as cold as death itself sighting along Big Thunder's stainless-steel barrel.

The two hundred and forty grains of Judgment turned Karim Yazid's skull into a bloody, collapsing thing and his life into nothing but a bad memory. The impact of the head shot lifted what was left of the hired Iranian assassin up off his feet and deposited him in an impossibly tangled heap of bones and dead flesh six feet away.

Mack Bolan rose to his feet, that smooth combat movement honed as always to a tight edge. The eyes were still iced. The .44 shifted from the dead man to the parked Mercedes.

Minera, still clad in his head honcho security guard outfit, emerged from behind the steering wheel. The guy was playing it very cool. He was not unaware of the fact that the .44 was now drawing a bead on the area directly between his eyes. But he kept his voice steady.

"Relax, Colonel. No need to point that thing at me. I figured I owed you for the help you gave me and my boys back in Potomac."

"Step forward," Bolan instructed, and Minera obeyed.

An angry sound that Bolan could not identify came from the back seat of the Mercedes.

Minera chuckled as Bolan approached and came up close. "The general isn't quite as appreciative as I am," he told Bolan. "He said that you were a good diversion. He wanted us to climb aboard the plane and beat it and let you and Yazid take care of each other. I didn't see it that way."

"I appreciate that, Minera."

"Sure. So, uh, now I helped you out, I figure we're even, right?"

"We are." The big guy nodded. But he did not lower the .44. "Now get the general and his bunch out here where I can talk with them. There's one more matter that needs attending to."

Minera glowered. "What is this? I help you out and you start pulling shit! The general's got a plane to catch."

"The general can catch his plane after we settle one last thing." Bolan's tone was colder than chilled steel, brooking no response save obedience. "I said to roust them out, Minera. Don't push me. You had a man killed last night. Before I even got to Potomac, some of your boys were trying to waste me over in Canal Park. I could remember all of that and blow you away very easily. *Capice?*"

Another heartbeat.

Minera seemed to weigh his options and decided that there was only one.

"Okay, we play it your way," he muttered.

Minera moved to the rear door of the Mercedes, on the side that was facing Bolan. He leaned inside to speak to the car's passengers.

The Executioner stood his ground, waiting, the .44 held down at hip level but ready.

There was a bustling movement from the back seat of the foreign car as the occupants prepared to follow orders and show themselves in the new morning sunlight.

The sunshine had warmed the air considerably by this time. But Bolan was still chilled to the bone as he psyched himself for the commencement of this drama's truly final act.

It was not over, no.

Not yet.

Not by any means.

18

In the distance, the STOL was taxiing toward them, maybe another three or four minutes away, Bolan estimated. Otherwise, the airfield in Bethesda belonged to the players in this drama. According to previous arrangement, Hal Brognola was holding his men in check at the entrances to the field until he was contacted by Bolan or saw Bolan go down.

Bolan did a quick scan of the four people who were lined up before the Mercedes, facing him.

General Eshan Nazarour sat in his wheelchair. The passenger quarters of the Mercedes evidently were equipped to accommodate it. He was swathed in a heavy blanket against the morning chill. He was trembling with rage.

"I insist that you allow me to leave on this aircraft, Colonel Phoenix," he snarled, with a nod toward the approaching STOL. "I appreciate your assistance. But your assistance is no longer necessary nor warranted. I must demand—"

Bolan did not hear him out. He looked at

Carol Nazarour, who stood between her crippled Iranian husband and Abbas Rafsanjani.

"Here's where you get off, lady," Bolan told the blonde. "If you still want to."

Carol started forward. "Thank you, Colonel. I'd be more than happy to—"

One of Nazarour's gnarled hands shot out from under the blanket and clasped itself around his wife's nearest wrist.

"Not so fast, my precious," he hissed. Then, to Bolan, "Any previous agreement that you and I may have had, Colonel, is null and void. My wife displeased me greatly a while ago when she called you from that restaurant and told you of our plans."

The STOL was drawing closer along the short airstrip. Bolan hoped that it carried only a pickup detail for Nazarour, that no one in the STOL would cause trouble. He did not want the situation to bother Hal and his men at the perimeter unnecessarily. . . .

He turned his attention to the general. He lifted the .44 and sighted in along a straightened arm at the man in the wheelchair.

The Executioner was not bluffing when he quietly said, "Release her, general, or I will blow your brains all over this airfield. Do as I say."

From a few feet away, Minera advised Nazarour in a stage whisper, "This guy is not bullshitting you, general. I'd say leave the lady behind."

"Sound advice," chimed in Rafsanjani.

Carol Nazarour was through being a passive observer of her own fate. She yanked her wrist from Nazarour's grasp, and he did not stop her.

"Let me go, you filthy pig!" she said vehemently. "I spit on you and what you are!"

And that is exactly what the hot-eyed blonde proceeded to do. The spit caught Nazarour squarely in the left eye. He reached up to wipe it away as his wife stalked over to stand beside Bolan.

Bolan looked at Minera. "You just gave the general some real good advice," he told the security chief. "Now I'll give you some. Take it if you want to live." He nodded at Nazarour. "Don't put anything on the line for this guy, Minera. He's a bigger hood than you are, and he doesn't give a shit if you live or die. If you want to get out of this thing, all you have to do is turn around and walk away. You killed one of your own men last night for the general because the guy was messing with the general's wife. Tony should've been smarter or more careful, but he was Mafia just like you are, so this time around, you get away with it. If you stay, I kill you. I'd rather not, after all we went through last night. But the choice is yours."

Minera looked at Bolan. He looked at the

mighty .44. He saw the expression, or lack of expression, in those frigid eyes.

He stalked off without a backward word or glance.

Which left Bolan and Carol Nazarour facing the general and Rafsanjani.

The STOL was some fifty yards away. Its approaching noise caused Bolan to raise his voice when he addressed Nazarour.

"I guess that about wraps it up, general. Except for the matter of who tipped off Yazid in the first place that you could be found in Potomac. And who arranged the arms smuggling.

"That would be the same person who planted the cyanide canisters in the gatehouse so that Yazid's men could break in so easily. The same person who killed your brother last night."

General Nazarour had been busy scanning the entrances to the airfield and the unmarked but obviously government sedans that were parked there. He looked back at the awesome American before him. His voice lost none of its animal strength as he raised it above the rumble of the approaching aircraft.

"The man who betrayed me is dead, Colonel Phoenix. He was my brother. Rafsanjani killed him."

Rafsanjani stepped closer to the general, offering a visible show of solidarity. "I saw Dr. Nazarour acting suspiciously," he said to

Bolan. "I followed him out of the house to the pool. He had a pocket radio of some kind. I came forward to question him. He whirled and attacked me like a madman. He fought. I killed him."

"My brother was a weak, loathesome person," sneered the general. "It doesn't surprise me, his betraying me as he did. Promise him drugs, and he would do anything."

"You should know," growled Bolan. "But it wasn't your brother who was pulling dirty tricks behind your back. It was Rafsanjani himself."

Rafsanjani's face twisted with surprise and rage.

Bolan read fear there too.

"What manner of madness is this?" The Peter Lorre voice carried a taut edge, was less sibilant.

But nothing fazed General Nazarour.

"What is the basis of your accusation, Colonel Phoenix?" he asked bluntly.

"Process of elimination mostly," Bolan announced, not taking his eyes off Rafsanjani. "I can't see Carol having the contacts to get word back to Tehran on where they could find you. Even if she had, you kept too close a watch on her for that. You knew about her escape tunnel. You knew about her lover. You even had Rafsanjani on top of her tonight when she tried to call me, even with all the pressure of being on the run as you were. So it wasn't Carol.

"And it wasn't Minera," he continued. "If Minera had set the thing up, he sure as hell wouldn't have put his life on the line as he did tonight in Potomac."

"And what of Medhi?" asked Nazarour. His voice was still emotionless, but he had about him the attitude of a man listening to and weighing Bolan's every word.

"Medhi did not betray you," said Bolan. "He was too dependent on you for drugs to ever break away. And he died heroically. He suspected Rafsanjani of informing on you. He warned me to beware of a traitor in your ranks. He wanted to protect you at all times, general. That is, he wanted to protect his drug source.

"But he wouldn't tell me names because I guess he was afraid of Rafsanjani, too. He probably went up to his room and got himself junked out. But instead of relaxing him, the junk just made him more paranoid. He must have decided that telling me about the traitor was not enough. He ended up stumbling outside again, looking for Rafsanjani with a stiletto. He was out of his league. Rafsanjani killed him instead."

The general turned slowly in his wheelchair and looked up at the man before him. "I await your denial, Abbas."

Rafsanjani only glared at Bolan. He seemed

wound in on himself, ready to explode outward, sizing his options.

"He can't deny it," Bolan growled. "It's all true. He has access to your funds, doesn't he?"

Nazarour's eyes did not leave Rafsanjani. "Abbas handles all of my finances. I trusted him implicity."

"Then that's his motive. He's greedy. He waited until the last minute. Then he contacted Tehran. And part of his price for fingering you was that he specify exactly when the hit was to be made. That allowed him to plant the cyanide canisters to nullify your security."

Rafsanjani had judged his options.

He moved.

He darted to the left, pawing beneath his jacket and coming up with a handgun. He brought the weapon up in Bolan's direction as he cut a sharp angle away from the man in black.

Bolan recognized the gun being pulled on him.

It was his own Beretta, loaned the night before.

The mighty AutoMag tracked upward and delivered one final load of thunder and death from Bolan's fist, spitting a 250-grain skull crusher that did just that. Rafsanjani never fired the Beretta. His near-headless body continued to run a few more paces before collapsing like a man pushing himself too hard and suddenly needing a long rest.

Bolan lowered the .44, holding it at his side. Carol Nazarour spoke first, staring at the latest kill in this night and dawn of slaughter.

"Oh, my God," came the lady's voice. "Thank God. . . ."

Bolan couldn't have agreed more.

He walked over and retrieved his Belle, which was still clasped in Rafsanjani's fingers. Then he walked back to the general.

Nazarour couldn't seem to take his eyes off the dead body of his aide.

"I was a fool," he said, and Bolan detected genuine regret in the Iranian's voice. "I have never trusted Medhi because of his addiction. Abbas played on this. He convinced me of my own brother's guilt. After I gave him shelter and trusted him. . . ."

"Rafsanjani saw his chance and he took it, and he didn't give a damn about trust," said Bolan. "That's something a man like you ought to understand, General." He nodded to the Sky Terrier, which had idled to a stop thirty feet away. "There's your plane. Get the hell out of our country."

The STOL's hatch and stairway were lowered. A man emerged. An Iranian. The guy wore civilian clothes, yet he had about him an unmistakably military bearing.

But there were no weapons in sight.

It was, yeah, only a pickup.

As Carol Nazarour had said: Thank God.

While Bolan and Carol watched, the man from the STOL crossed to the general and offered a sharp salute, which Nazarour returned. The general spoke something in his native tongue.

The man nodded, stepped behind the wheelchair, and wheeled Nazarour around and off toward the STOL, which they boarded.

General Nazarour never looked back at the woman who had been his wife.

Moments later, the strange craft dramatically lifted off the ground, banking in an easterly direction toward the ocean.

Probably toward a waiting yacht, thought Bolan.

Toward another siege against the world.

19

Bolan was thinking that he should have blown the man away. In a different time, maybe he would have done so. A guy like Nazarour should not be given a diplomatic cloak to legitimize his savagery. But he was wearing one this time, and Bolan had to honor it.

The general's STOL disappeared beyond the hospital district skyline, as though into some new slice of time and space, leaving the realities behind. Bolan sighed and allowed his mind to play with those realities for a moment. Minera, too, had disappeared.

Unmarked federal sedans were clustered at both entrances to the bloodied airfield, awaiting their cue for entry. A hushed crowd of civilians was beginning to form beyond the fence, drawn by the gunfire.

And, as though from another time and place, Carol Nazarour approached, still wrapped in the same leather coat she'd been wearing when Bolan first saw her—was it just last night? Another time and place, yeah. Aeons ago.

Many dead men ago. She told him in a breathless little voice, "Thank you, Colonel. Many, many thanks."

Bolan smiled at her with eyes only as he lifted the transceiver to his head and spoke into it. "This is Stony Man One. All clear here."

Brognola's somber tones bounced back instantly. "Okay. We're moving. Where's Minera?"

"Gave 'im a white flag," Bolan told him. "Guess he took it."

There was urgency in Brognola's voice as he replied, "You may want to take it back. I've got two words for you: Arnie Farmer."

Arnesto "the Farmer" Castiglione had been the big boss of the Eastern seaboard from Jersey to Florida when Bolan executed him during the Mafia wars.

Bolan's voice was cold and clipped as he responded to that. "Cordon the field. Give me a sieve as fine as you can manage."

"You got it," Brognola assured him.

Bolan told the lady. "Stay put, right here. They'll take care of you." He brushed her cheek lightly with the back of his hand, then bent to kiss her quickly.

"Thank you again," she whispered.

But Bolan did not hear. He was already moving swiftly across the battlefield, seeking a rendezvous with his past.

Time out of sync, yeah. That warp of space and time was right here, right now. Minera was carrying it, not Nazarour. And Mack Bolan intended to find it.

Arnesto Castiglione, or "Arnie Farmer," had been one of those primal American savages who built an empire with jungle cunning, sheer ferocity, and untempered greed. Sometimes also known as "the Lord of Baltimore," the Farmer had "domesticated" the entire U.S. East Coast from New Jersey south by the time Mack Bolan first came onto the guy. He was one of the strongest Mafia bosses in the country, virtually uncontested by the law or the lawless, and he had become accustomed to the kind of absolute power that turns politicians and industrialists, bankers and businessmen, labor and management alike, into puppets.

The common wisdom of the day had Arnie destined to become *Capo di tutti Capi*, or Boss of All the Bosses—and probably he would have, except for Bolan's explosive entry into the equation.

He removed the Farmer early in the Mafia wars, but so strong was the man's empire, so well stocked with able and ambitious lieutenants who kept rising to power, that it was among the last to fall into disarray under Bolan's determined assaults.

And, of course, the very turf now beneath

Bolan's feet had been the heartland of the Castiglione empire. So it had required no great leap of imagination to understand Brognola's terse two-word report concerning the status of Minera as some dangerous echo of the Arnie Farmer empire.

Bolan caught up with the guy inside an A&E hangar. He was stumbling into a pair of white service coveralls that had just been removed from the freshly dead body of a mechanic who unluckily had found himself in a sound wave of that echo from the past.

"Forget it," Bolan frigidly advised the Mafioso.

Minera's gaze came up slowly, traveling the full length of the impressive "colonel," halting finally in a confrontation with icy blue eyes. He dropped the coveralls and kicked them away without breaking that eye contact.

"What's your problem, soldier?" the Mafioso asked quietly, a whole new voice and an entirely new personality behind it.

"You put on a convincing show," Bolan told him. "Good enough to fool me all the way. It would have worked...except the warp caught up with you."

Minera was moving slowly, carefully maneuvering toward a combat stance. "What warp?" he asked coldly. "I don't know what you're saying."

Both men's weapons were holstered. Minera

was trying to square off, his right hand hovering stiffly at the butt of his pistol, but Bolan kept moving with him.

"I'm saying, Minnie, that you call the shots for Nazarour."

The guy laughed without humor as he replied. "Bullshit. I just ran the joint for 'im. But so what if I do? What's it to you?"

"Could be a whole lot," Bolan said quietly. "Depends on what it is to you."

A slow smile began at the corners of Minera's mouth, a smile that never quite reached the eyes. He said, "Okay. Maybe I could use a guy like you at this end. You got Pentagon connections?"

The weird little dance was still going on between the two men. "Better than that," Bolan told him.

"How much better?"

"Best you can get. But I'm not interested in a weekly envelope, pal."

The dance halted and Minera laughed, genuinely. "So maybe we'll talk a percentage...if you can really deliver."

"A percentage of what?" Bolan quietly inquired.

"The whole damn world maybe," said Arnie Farmer's heir. "The general will deliver a piece of the Middle East. Soon as he does that, other pieces will fall in line."

"Which others?"

Minera scowled. "We'll talk about it later."

"We'll talk about it right now," Bolan told him.

"Or what?" Minera sneered.

"Or you get what Arnie got," Bolan said coldly.

"What?"

"You heard it. I'm the one that wiped him, Minnie."

"What?" The dance began again. Minera wiped his lips with the back of his left hand and chewed on a knuckle for a moment. "What'd you say?"

"I also wiped Billy Garante and Mario Cuba."

"Santelli?" Minera whispered. "Damon? La Carpa?"

"Them, too," Bolan confirmed softly.

Minera went for his piece then. He did not quite get there. Bolan delivered a judo kick to the elbow of his gun arm. It popped audibly and fell helplessly away, dangling in numb paralysis. Minera groaned and tried to throw a punch with his left. Bolan went inside of it and broke the arm against his chest, then pinned the howling Mafioso to the wall with a hand at his throat. That stopped the bleating. Minera's eyes were rolling wildly as he struggled to pull air through his constricted larynx.

Bolan eased off just a bit, enough to allow those dangling feet to find a little purchase.

"You're Bolan!" the Mafioso gasped.

"You got it, pal."

"I thought you were—"

"I'm not. But maybe you are. What's the scam with Nazarour?"

Minera's eyes were reflecting the horror of a brutal soul at Judgment Day. It could have been the realization of a nightmare shared with all of his ilk, a dread that supposedly had found remission in the flaming wreck of a GMC motorhome in Central Park one rainy night, the night when Mack Bolan officially "died." Those horrified eyes were searching for an out, for some rebuttal to the awful truth. They found no comfort whatsoever in the icy stare of this adversary. Minera groaned with pain and said, "Look, I don't...I was just...it's all bullshit. I got nothing with the general."

"Then you can die with clean hands," Bolan suggested. He returned the pressure, lifting the guy away from earth again.

Those eyes bugged and rolled, and spittle formed at the lips as Minera tried to squeeze airless words past them.

Bolan gave him just enough adjustment and said, "I didn't catch that, Minnie."

"I said okay," the Mafioso sputtered. "It's like you say. I call the shots."

"For what?"

"For the new thing. We're pulling it together again."

"Starting where?"

"Africa."

"Uh huh," Bolan said softly. "What's the territory?"

Minera's groaning response was unintelligible.

"Say it again," Bolan commanded.

Minera croaked, "Military stuff."

"Nukes," Bolan decided.

"Whatever." Minera tried to clear his throat but could not. The eyes rolled as he continued. "I'm dying, huh? You're killing me. Let off."

"There are worse crimes than killing," Bolan told him coldly. "Letting off sometimes, for example."

"Huh?"

"One death against thousands, Minnie—maybe even millions. How do we balance that?"

"I guess I don't get you," Minera groaned.

Bolan reapplied the pressure as he told the dying man, "I guess you do." He lifted the guy completely off the floor, by the throat, and quietly held him there through the final agonized struggle, then slowly lowered the lifeless body to the floor of the hangar.

Brognola came through the door while Bolan

was verifying the lack of life signs. The fed turned about quickly and went back out. Bolan joined him just outside the hangar and told him, "Arnie Farmer is dead again. How many times do I have to cancel the guy, Hal?"

"Let's hope this was the last one," Brognola replied with a tired sigh.

"Don't bet any lives on it," Bolan said. "The shit machines have an amazing ability to reassemble themselves. Even from the grave. Nazarour has to be stopped."

"Why?"

"I believe Minera was pulling together a combine to supply nuclear weapons to the Mideast. Someone over there obviously wants them very bad. Minera said Africa. I would have to guess Libya. And that could be only the beginning."

"Of the end," Brognola commented.

"Wherever and however, Nazarour is probably the central figure."

Brognola stared sadly at the ground as he tried to bring it all together in his mind. "Hell," he growled, "we turned the guy loose. Now he's free as a bird."

"Maybe not," Bolan replied. "Can you get me a link to Stony Man?"

Brognola's eyes were question marks as he jerked a thumb toward his vehicle. "Channel A," he explained, referring to the two-way radio.

Bolan strode to the vehicle, punched in the linkage to Stony Man Farm, and devoted some five minutes to quiet radio conversations with several different individuals. Brognola studiously avoided the vehicle during that period, approaching only when it was obvious that the Striker's business had been concluded.

"I'll settle for a hint," the fed told the big man in black.

Bolan lit a cigarette and took a deep pull at it, exhaling the smoke with a tired sigh. Then he gave the fed his "hint" for the day. "A STOL aircraft was observed attempting a rendezvous with a large yacht fifty miles off the coast. Funny thing happened, though. It suddenly burst into flames and fell into the sea several miles short of its goal. No way could there have been any survivors."

Brognola lit a fresh cigar while he assimilated that bit of intelligence. "Strange things do happen," he commented after a moment. "How, uh, how'd you get that?"

Bolan smiled thinly, dropped his cigarette to the ground, and crushed it beneath his foot. "Grimaldi told me."

Brognola nervously shifted his weight and said, "He, uh—you, uh...."

Bolan said, "Yeah. We thought it would be a good idea if he flew a bit of coastal cover during all this. He, uh, borrowed an F-16. You know, any eventuality."

The fed chuckled and stepped into his vehicle. "I don't know what the hell you're talking about," he said cheerily. "My official report is going to say that all mission goals were fully met."

"Or exceeded," Bolan suggested. "You could say that."

And, yeah, you could say that.

THE PRESIDENT

HB — Urgent POW situation
has arisen in Vietnam. This
one for Phoenix. Confirm ASAP
personally for special support and
traffic codes. Further information
to follow immediately.

OPERATIONAL IMMEDIATE
FR WHITE HOUSE/BROGNOLA 211440Z
TO PHOENIX/STONYMAN
BT
MISSION ALERT X NEW INTEL SUGGESTS
POSSIBLE BREAK VIETNAM/MIA QUESTION X CIA
CONFIRMATION MISSION FRUSTRATED AND
STATUS NOW CRITICAL X PHOENIX STYLE
PENETRATION MISSION WITH ONLY MINIMAL
SUPPORT SEEMS INDICATED X COURIER NOW
EN ROUTE STONYMAN WITH INFOPAC X TOPMAN
REQUESTS IMMEDIATE ATTENTION AND ADVICE
NSC/URGENT BASIS
BT
211440Z
EOM

OPERATIONAL IMMEDIATE
FR STONYMAN OPS 211510Z
TO BROGNOLA/WH/WASHDC
BT
STONYMAN ONE CONTACTED IN FLIGHT RE UR
211440Z X CONCURS X REQUESTS DIVERT
COURIER RENDEZVOUS CIA FIELD OPS BANGKOK
ALL SOONEST AND SLATE REDLINE SUPPORT
PHOENIX MISSION THAT AREA X APRIL SENDS AND
PS HE SOUNDS A BIT TOO DAMNED HAPPY WITH THIS
ONE
BT
211510Z
EOM

MACK BOLAN

THE EXECUTIONER 43

appears again in
Return to Vietnam
DON PENDLETON

**Coming in July
from Gold Eagle Books**

**Following is a preview of this stunning
new story in the saga of Mack Bolan,
a.k.a. Col. John Phoenix**

MACK BOLAN

Return to Vietnam

It still hurts: 57,692 U.S. servicemen were killed in the jungles of Vietnam; more than 500,000 were wounded, more than 100,000 of them seriously disabled. Three million Americans served their country in that bitter and terrible thirteen-year conflict.

Today, word is leaking out of Vietnam regarding American fighting men still being held captive in Southeast Asia. Each month new reports indicate the sighting of American POWs. The Vietnam War was officially over May 7, 1975, yet current estimates number nearly 2,500 Americans unaccounted for and presumed dead, missing or imprisoned.

Most of these cases have been administratively reviewed by the U.S. government, resulting in a PFD (Presumptive Finding of Death). But during the past two years there have been approximately one thousand reports—including three hundred first-hand sightings—of U.S. POWs still being detained inside Vietnam.

Recently a Swedish journalist came back with news of American prisoners, shackled hand and foot, being forced to work on a Viet railroad. *"Tell the world we're here! Tell them not to forget us!"* is what he heard.

*   *   *

At last he was back in Vietnam.

"The boat on the left—*take 'em!*"

Bolan's finger caressed the AKM's trigger.

The weapon commenced blasting and bucking in his grip. It lit up the pitch darkness with silver strobe flashes, spitting a dozen blistering, tightly patterned rounds that took out the spotlight on the approaching boat even before it could swing around to take in Bolan's sampan.

Mack's allies opened fire with their Type 56s at the other boat on their right. Its spotlight, too, disintegrated. The battle zone was thrown into total darkness again.

Bolan set down his AKM close beside him, then reached into his pouch. He withdrew one of the M34 incendiary frag grenades.

He yanked the pin with his teeth and

heaved the missile at Patrol Boat Number One.

The M34 carries only a four-to-five-second fuse. It hit the deck of the enemy boat with no time for any of the enemy onboard to reach the thing and toss it away.

The grenade blasted the night wide open—and exploded several bodies along with it, igniting the night with a brightness tenfold greater than the rifles had. The boat lifted momentarily from the water, wreathed in a sheet of flaring death.

Bolan heard splashes quite near him as airborne parts of people plopped into the water.

Now an angry exchange of automatic-weapons fire was clattering between his friends and Patrol Boat Number Two. Bolan swung the AKM back into action. He kept the weapon on automatic and swept the deck of the crippled boat with a wide figure-eight pattern, sending a hail of 7.62 tumblers on their own unique Search & Destroy.

Only one RPD and two AK-47s were returning fire from this boat.

Bolan again shifted the AKM and reached into his pouch. He would get his taste of overkill now, though he knew well enough that no amount of destruction could avenge the atrocities of these fiendish creeps.

The big American produced his second M34, tugged the pin and lobbed it as accurately as the first.

Another direct hit.

The blinding explosion eliminated the patrol boat's cabin entirely, sending chunks of debris and human anatomy billowing into the simmering air.

There was no more firing from either boat. Only silence.

"Let's move on," commanded Mack Bolan.

Watch for *Return to Vietnam*, Executioner #43, wherever paperback books are sold—July, 1982.

Coming in June
from Gold Eagle

AN EXECUTIONER SERIES

ABLE TEAM

by Don Pendleton and Dick Stivers

In Able Team #1: *Tower of Terror*, and
Able Team #2: *The Hostaged Island*

Bolan's Death Squad is reborn at last

Tower of Terror—features the invasion of Wall Street's giant WorldFiCor Tower. Early one Saturday morning, the building is seized by a savage group of psychos from Puerto Rico, armed to the teeth with weaponry purchased with enormous sums of embezzled U.S. funds. The terrorists learn how badly they have miscalculated when Able Team hits the street!

The Hostaged Island—tells the story of Catalina Island's darkest day, when the rich playground off the coast of Los Angeles is host to more than seventy filthy motorcycle hoodlums who abuse and imprison seventeen hundred innocent folk in a bomb-primed casino. Again, Able Team shows the lawbreakers the depth of their mistake!